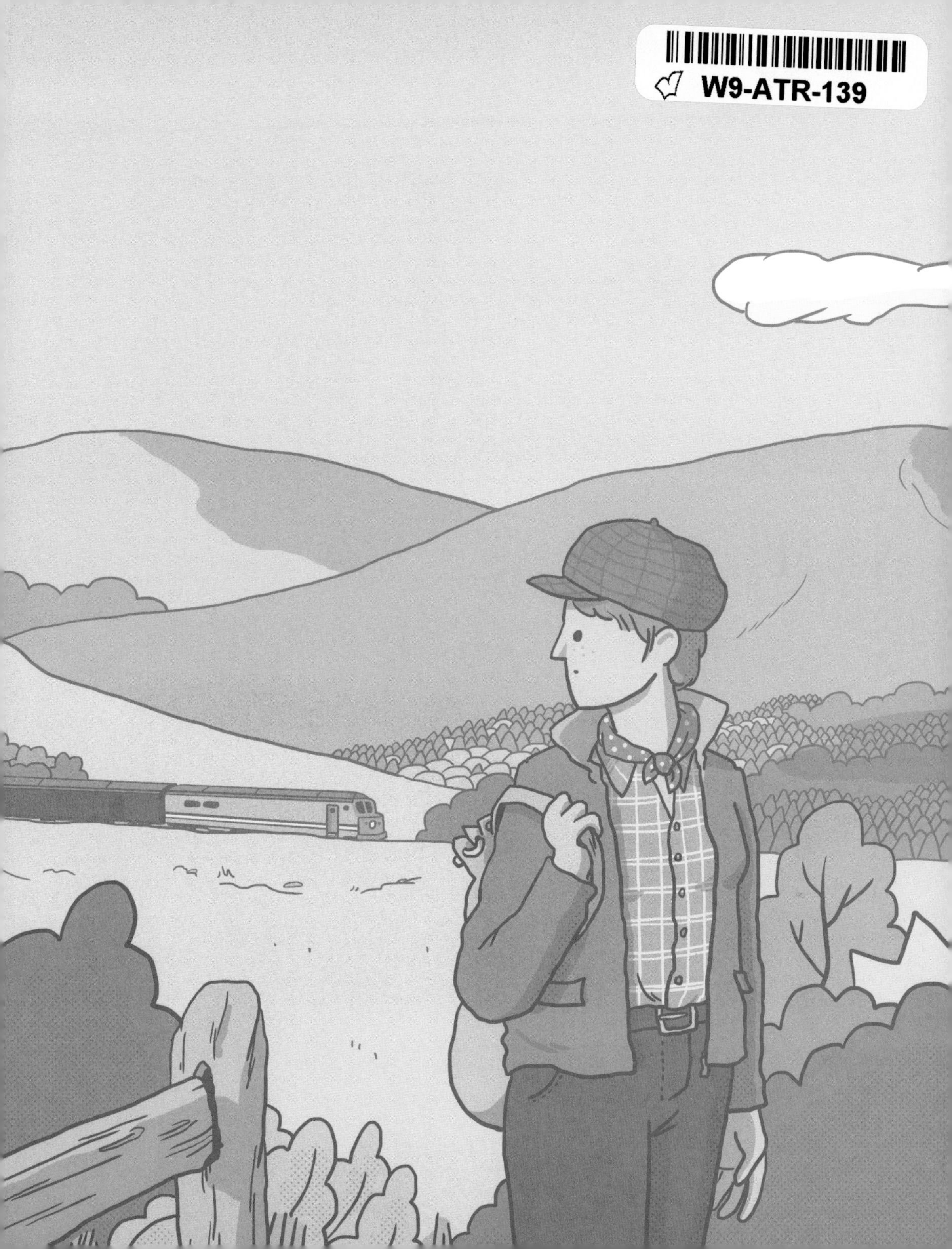

HOBO MOM

Charles Forsman - Max de Radiguès

The authors would like to thank the teams at Editions Delebile and the Hamelin Cultural Association. Special thanks as well to Bianca Bagnarelli and Lorenzo Ghetti.

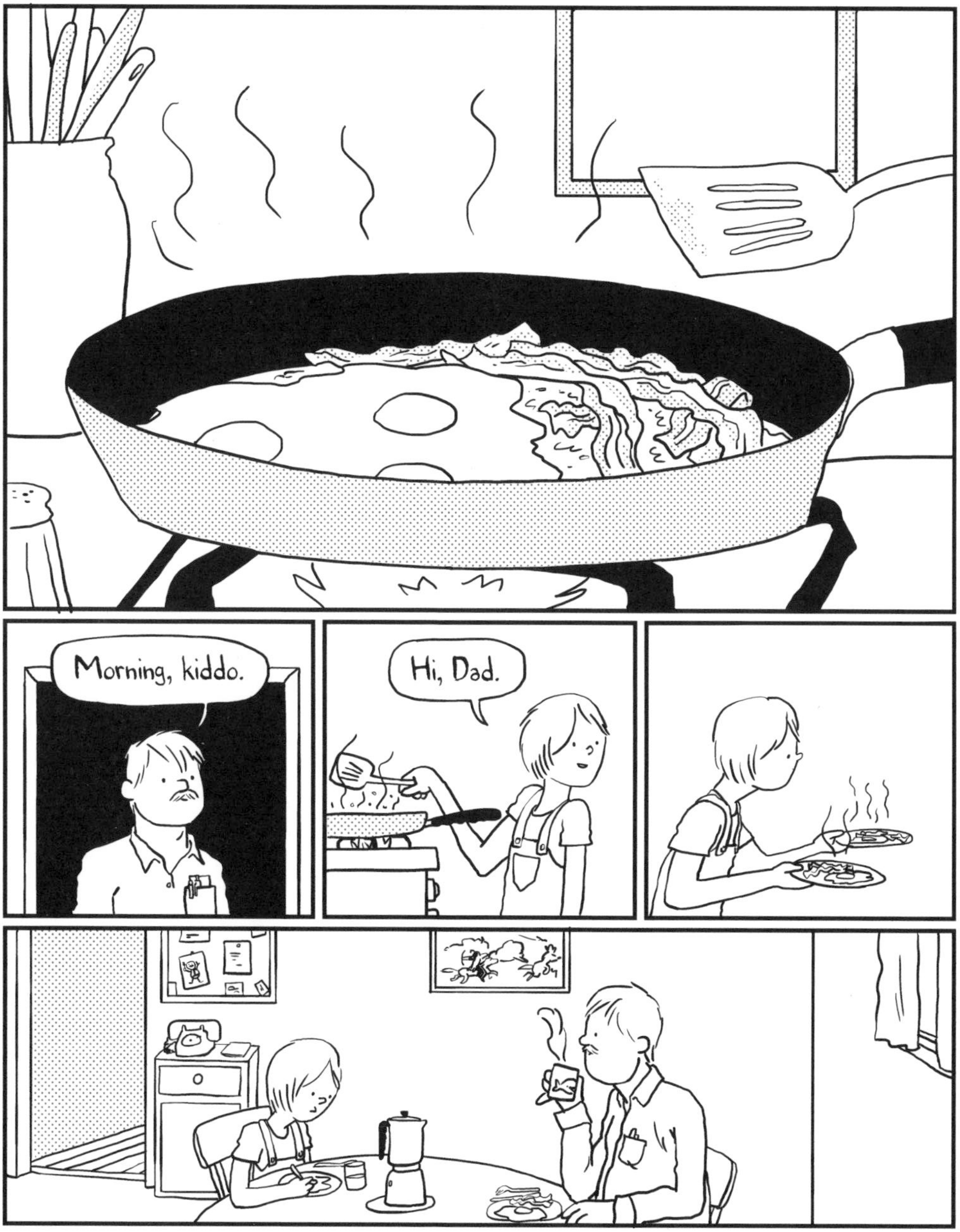
Morning, kiddo.
Hi, Dad.

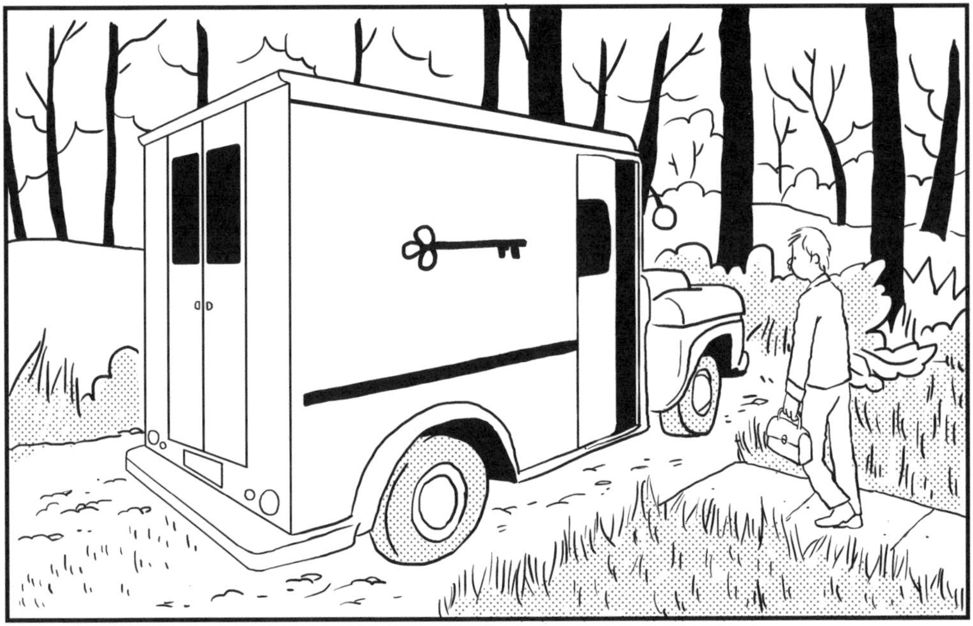

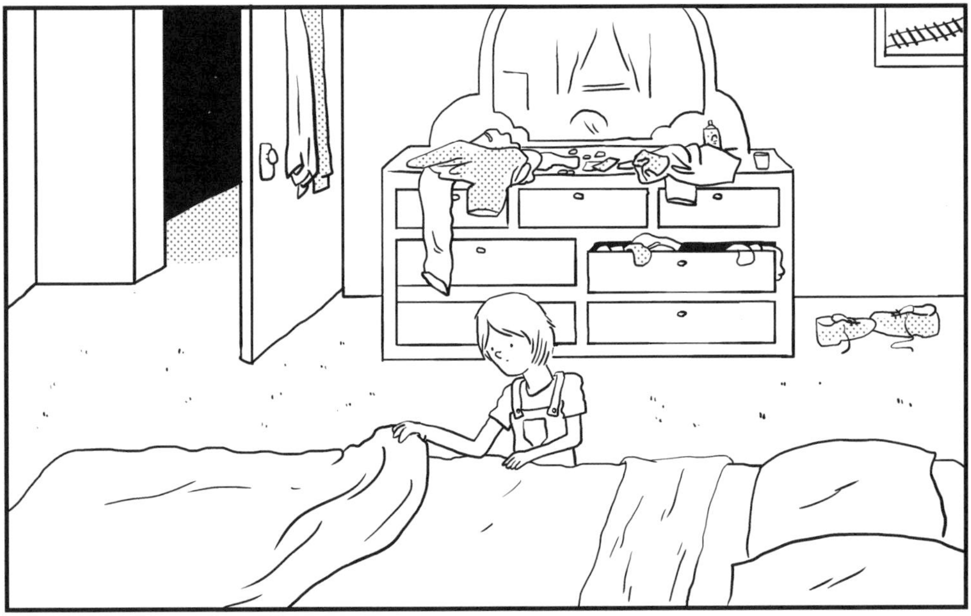

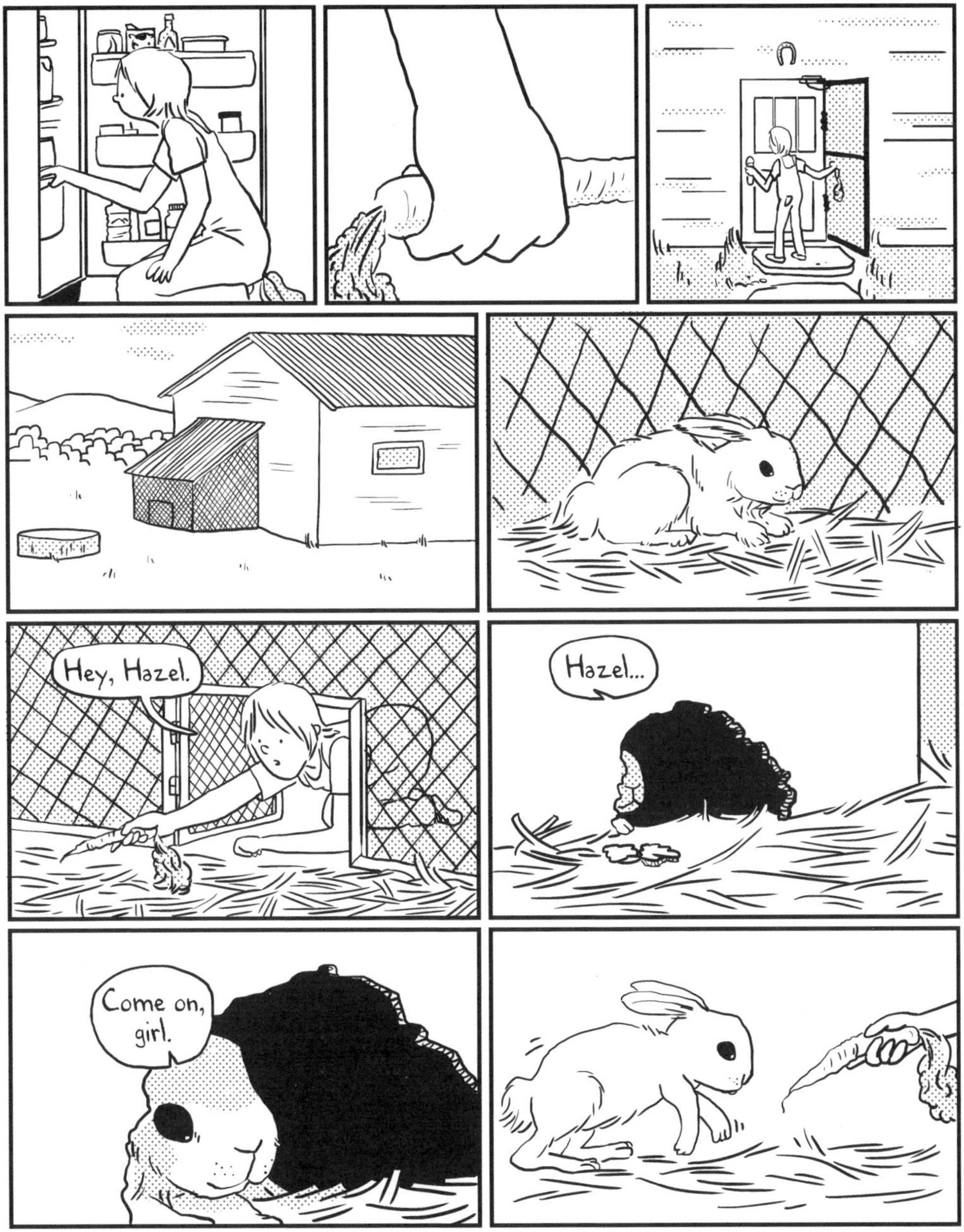
Hey, Hazel.
Hazel...
Come on, girl.

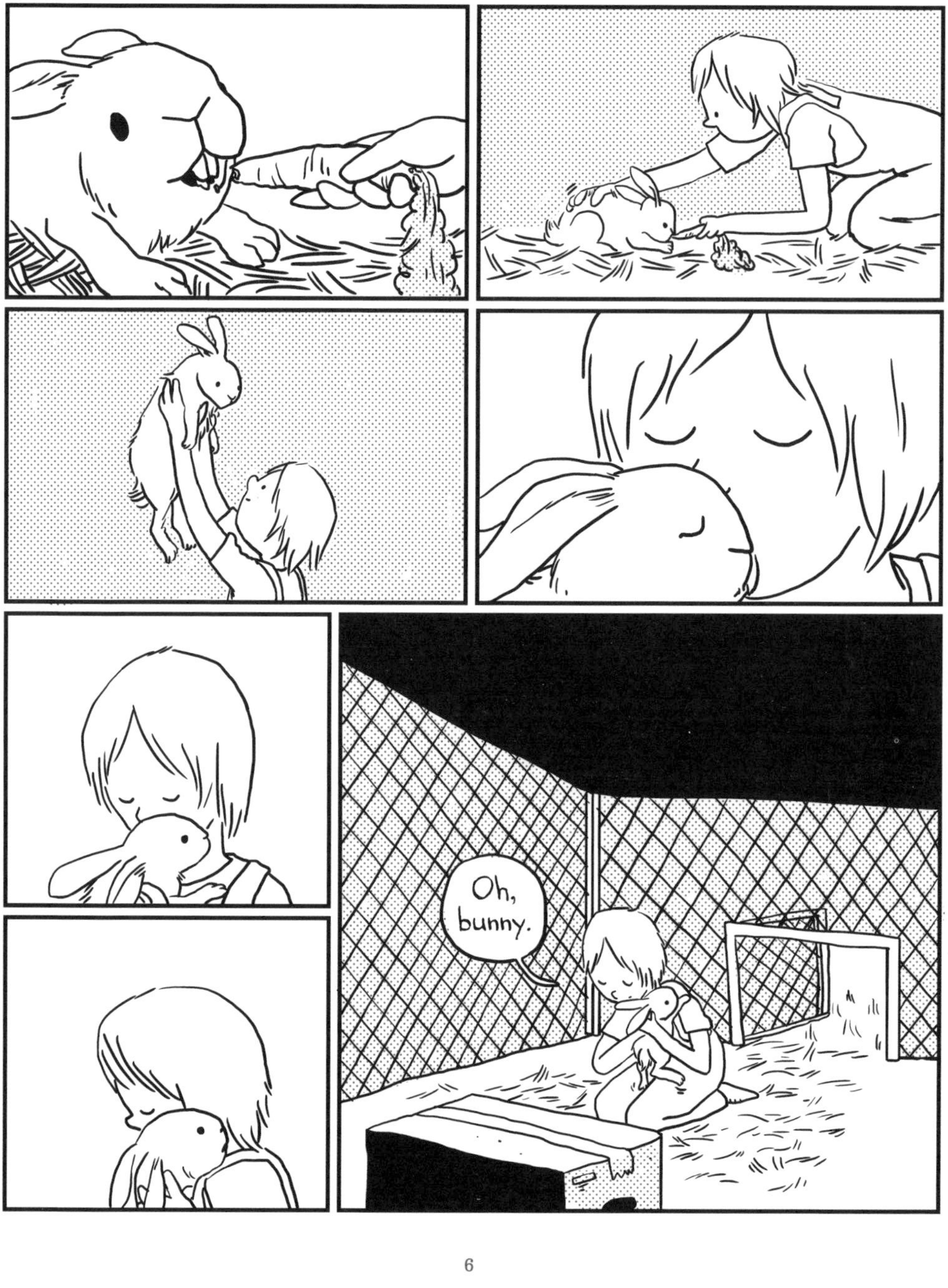
Oh, bunny.

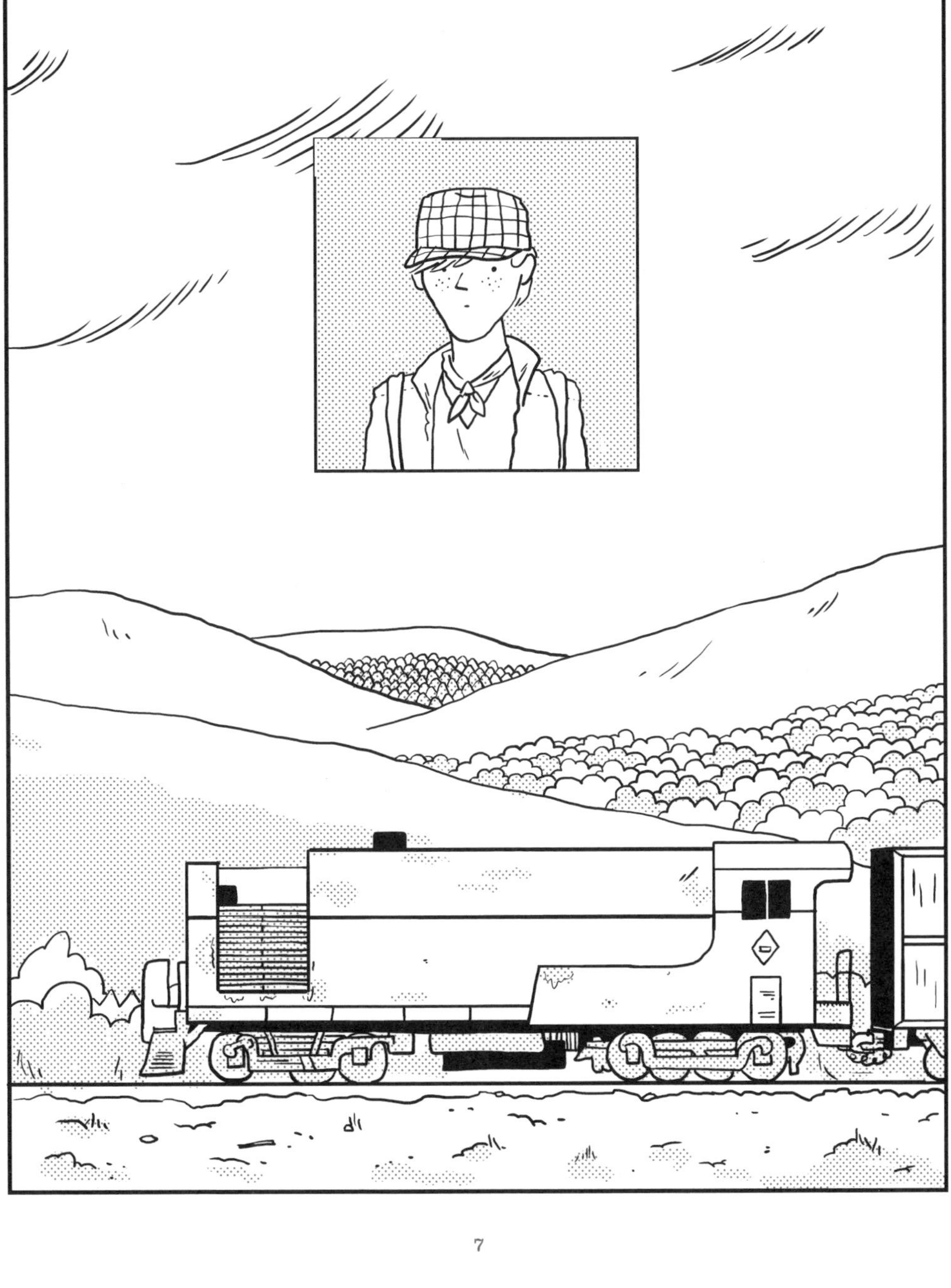

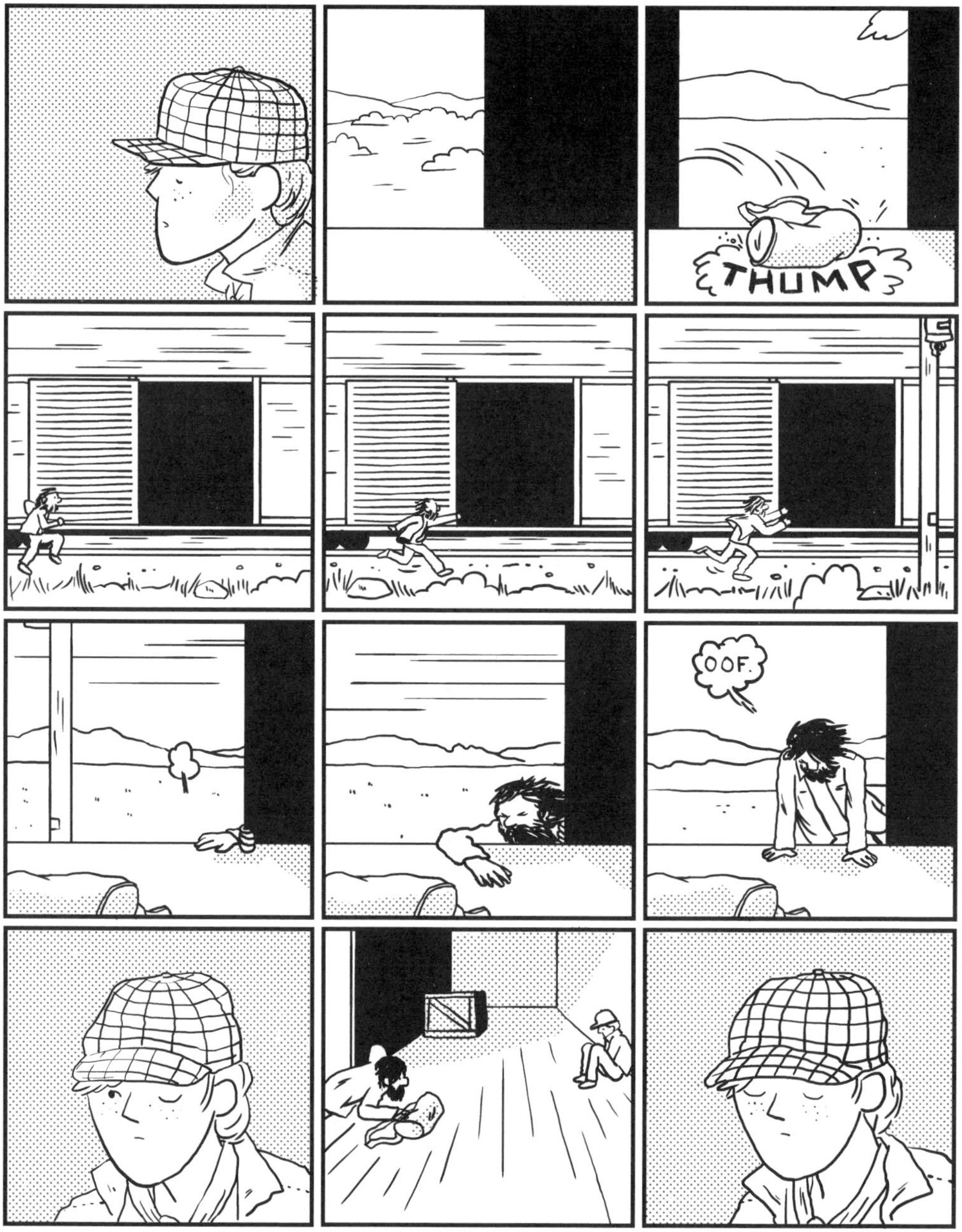
THUMP
OOF.

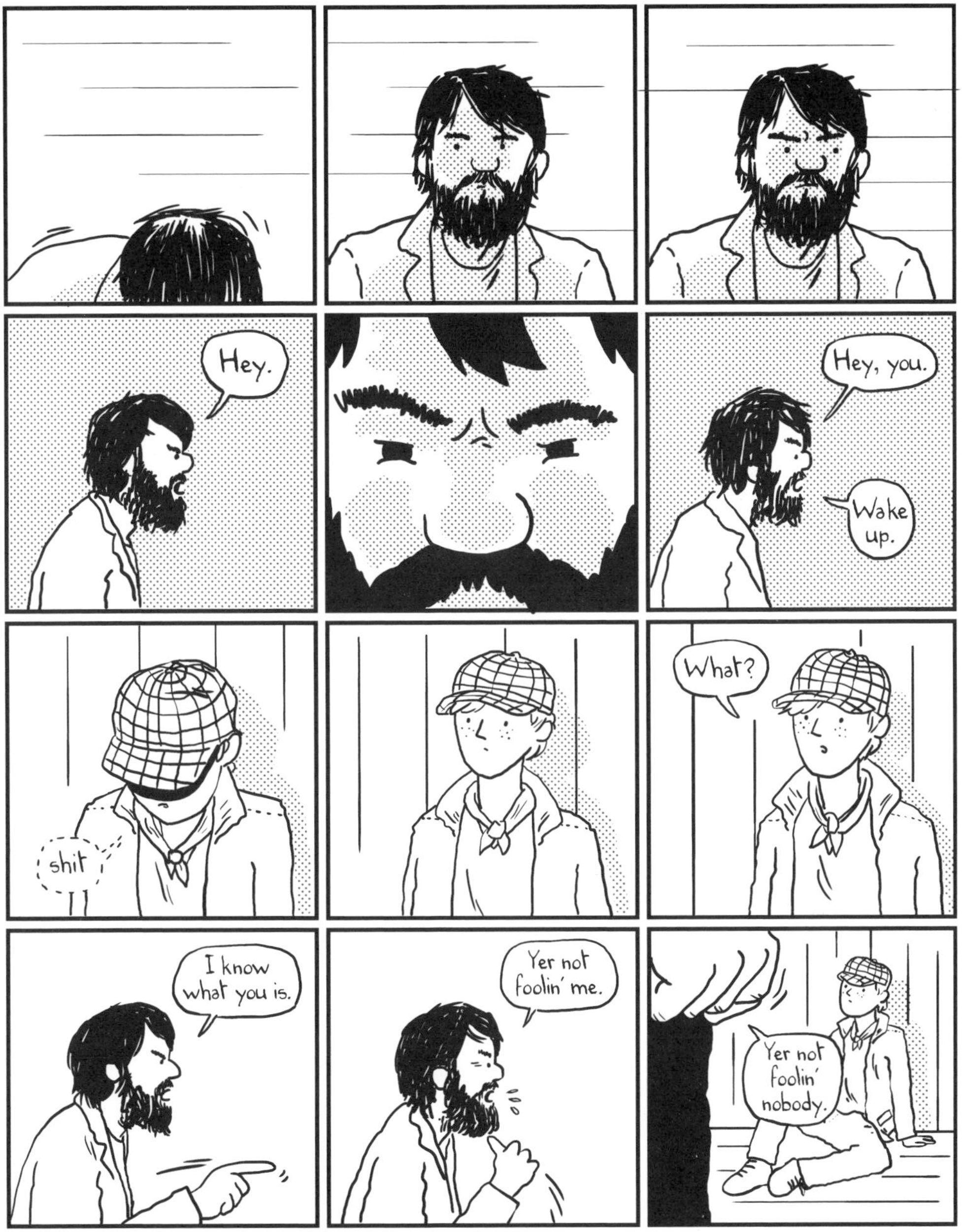
Hey.
Hey, you.
Wake up.
shit
What?
I know what you is.
Yer not foolin' me.
Yer not foolin' nobody.

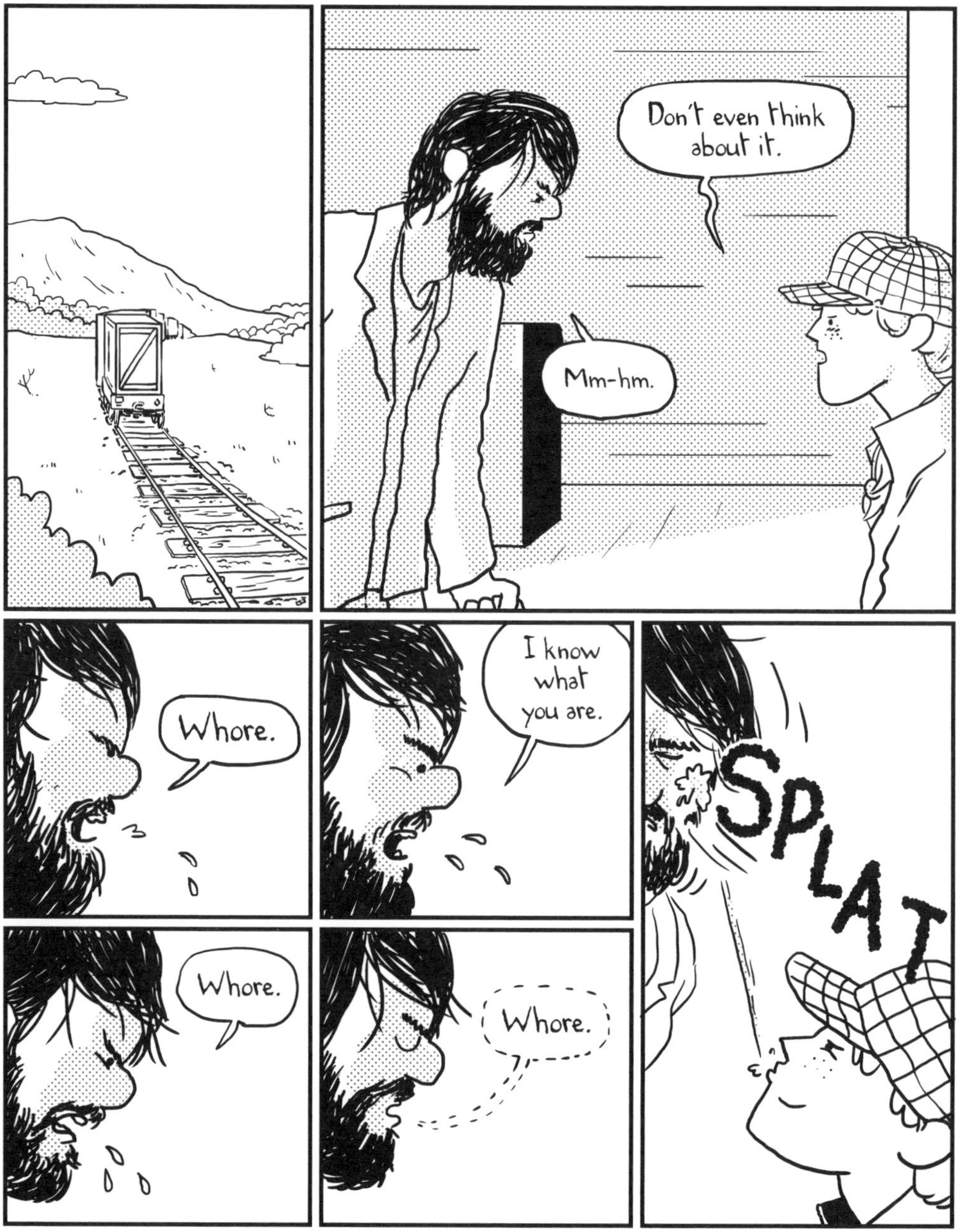
Don't even think about it.
Mm-hm.
Whore.
I know what you are.
SPLAT
Whore.
Whore.

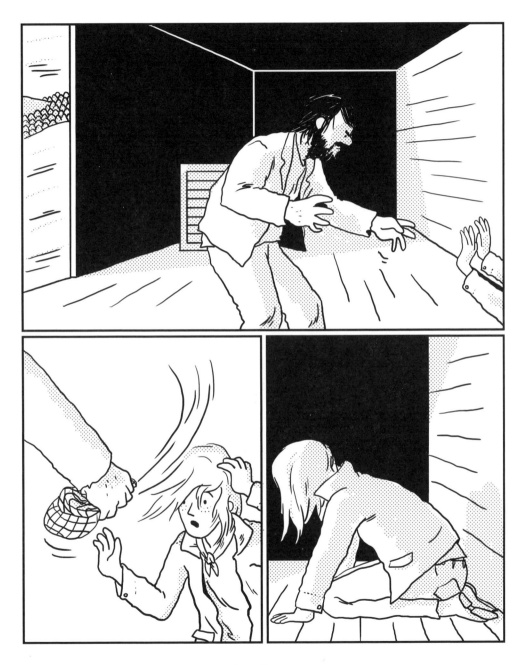

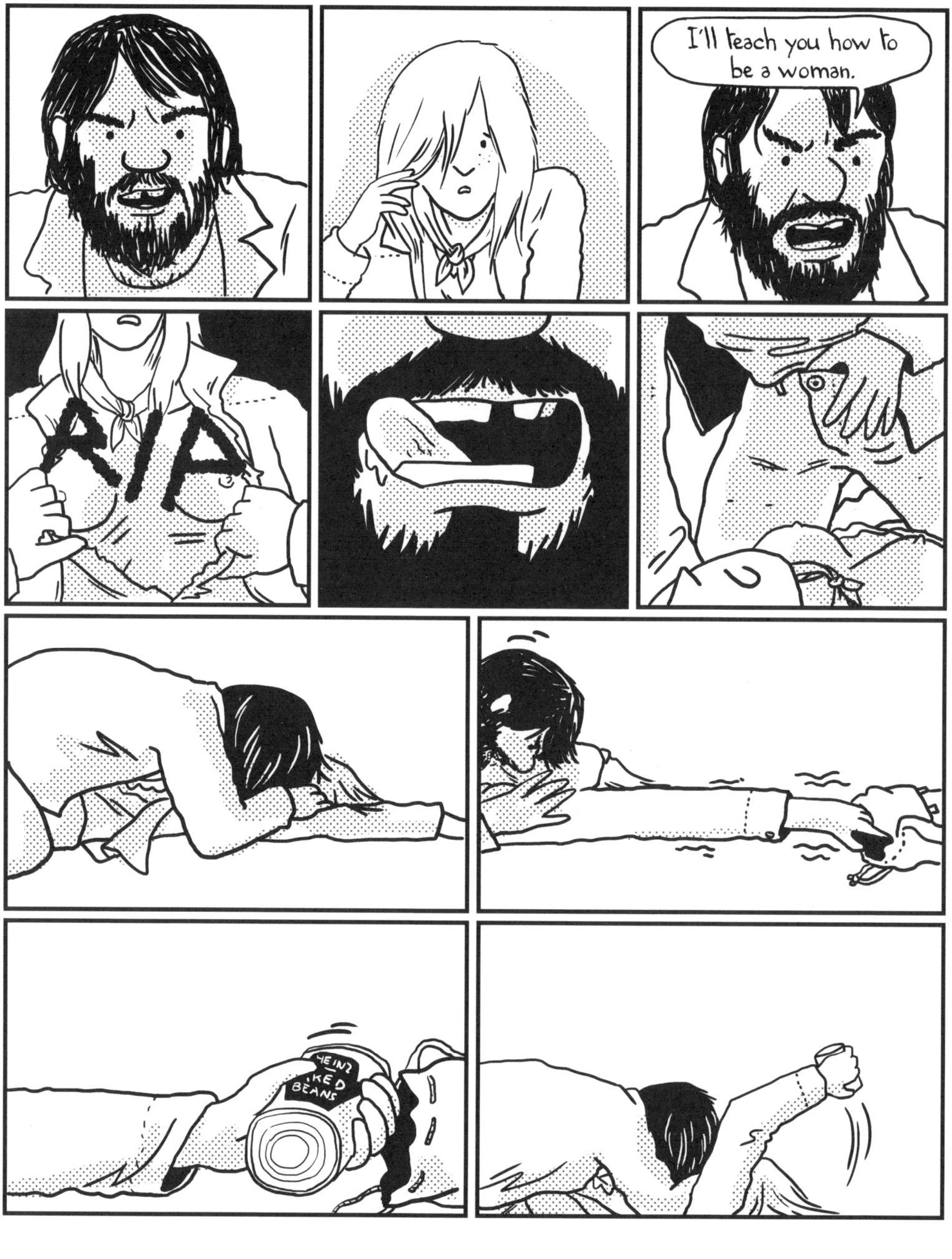
I'll teach you how to be a woman.
RIP
HEINZ
KED
BEANS

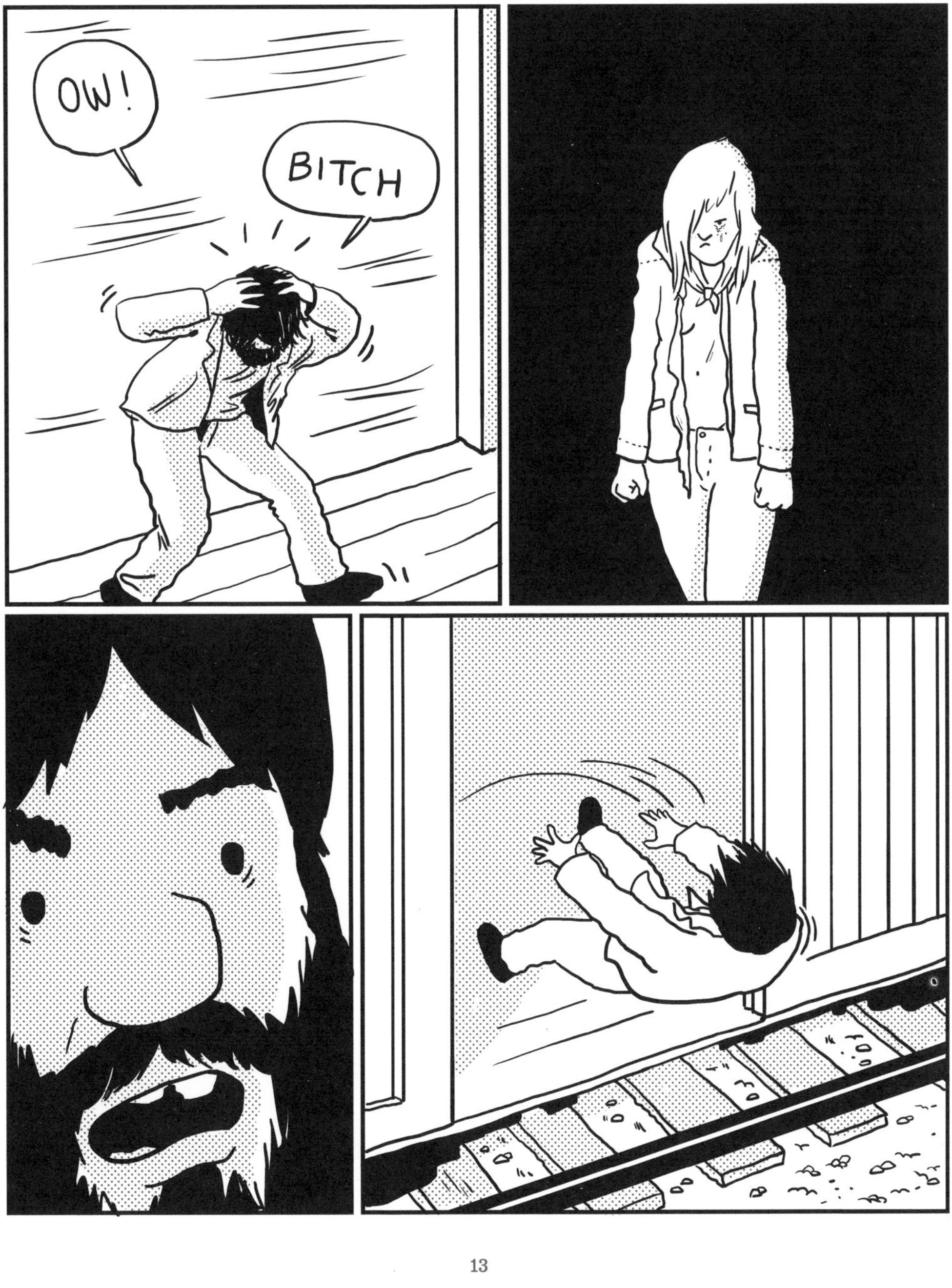
OW!
BITCH

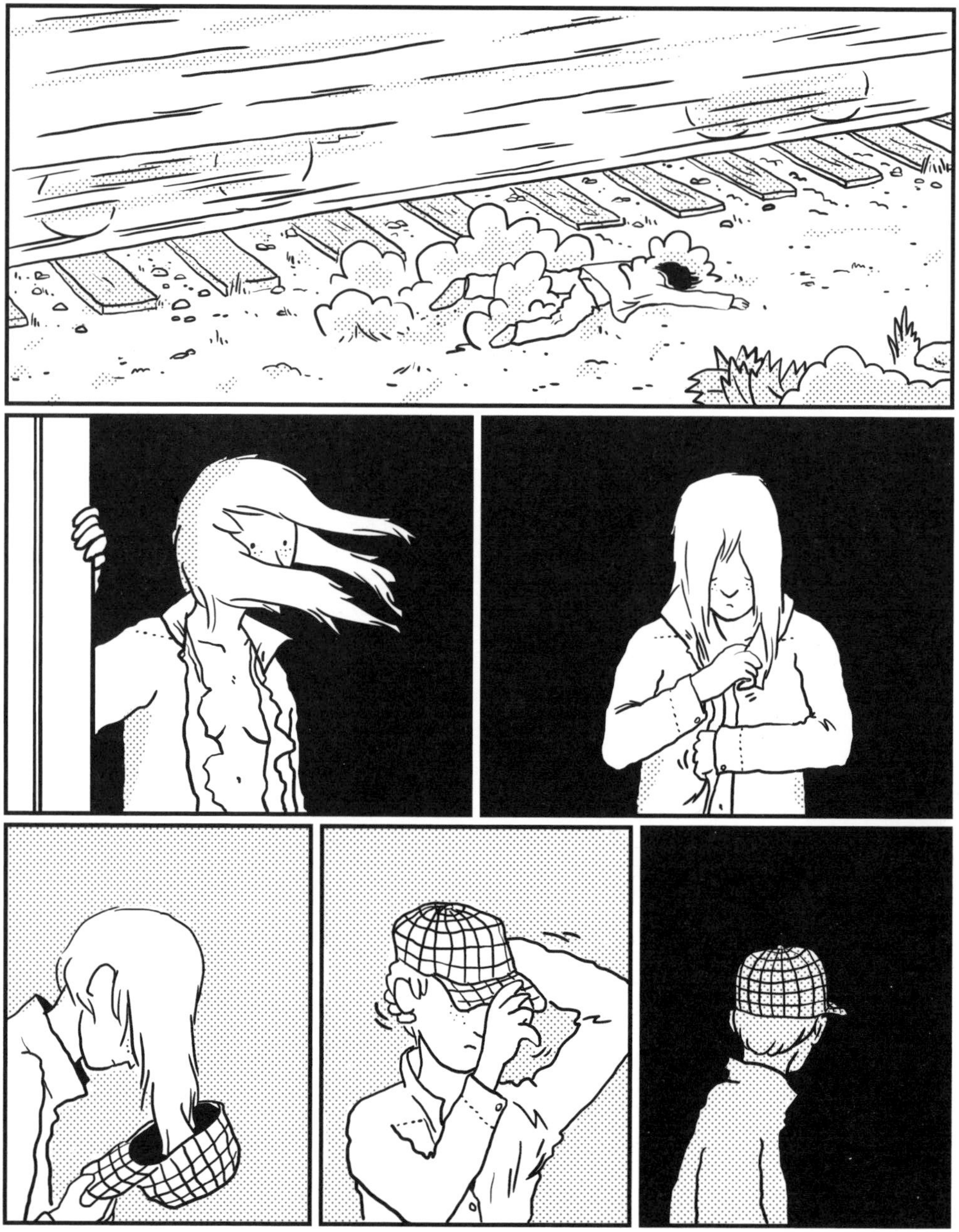

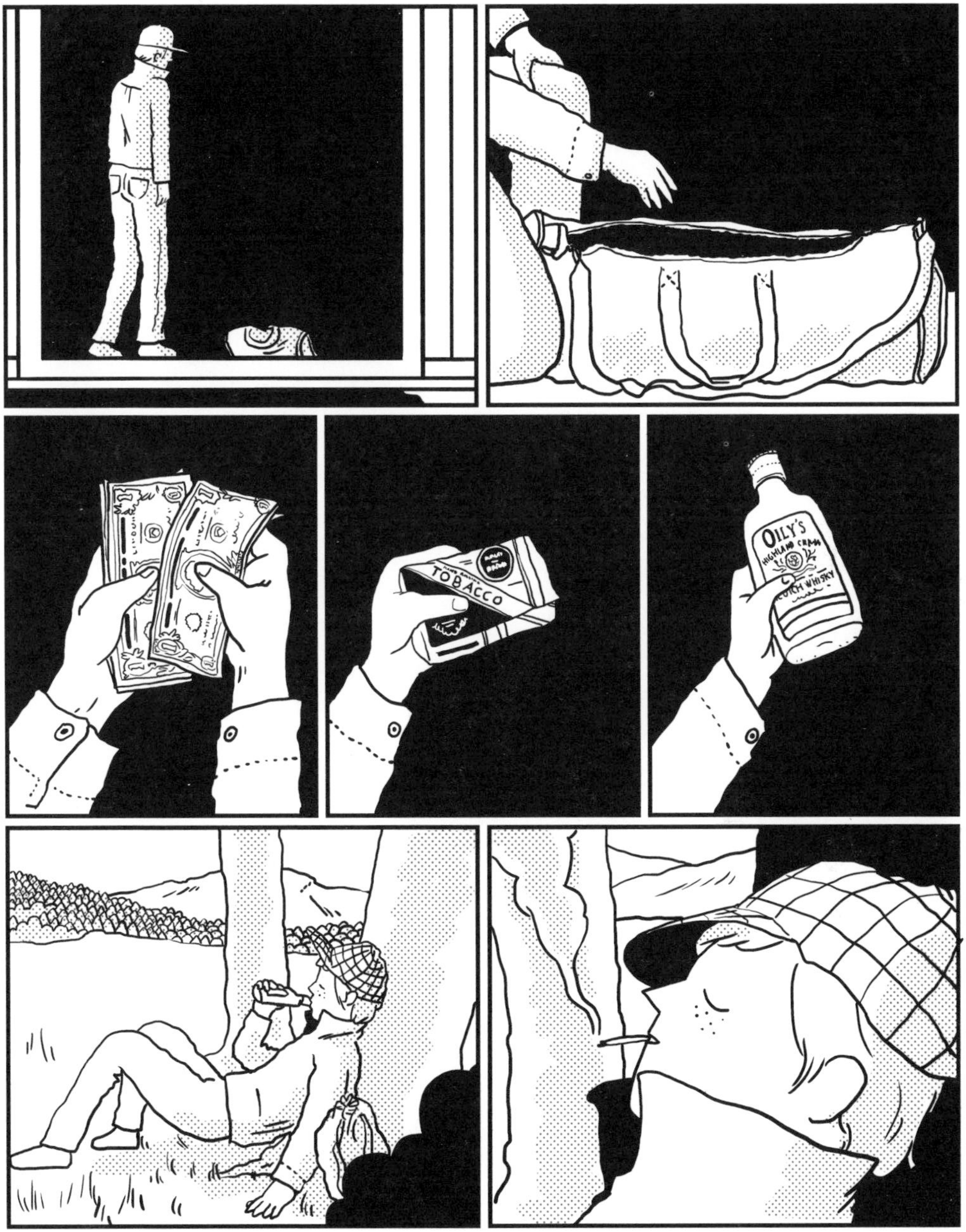
TOBACCO
OILY'S
HIGHLAND
WHISKY

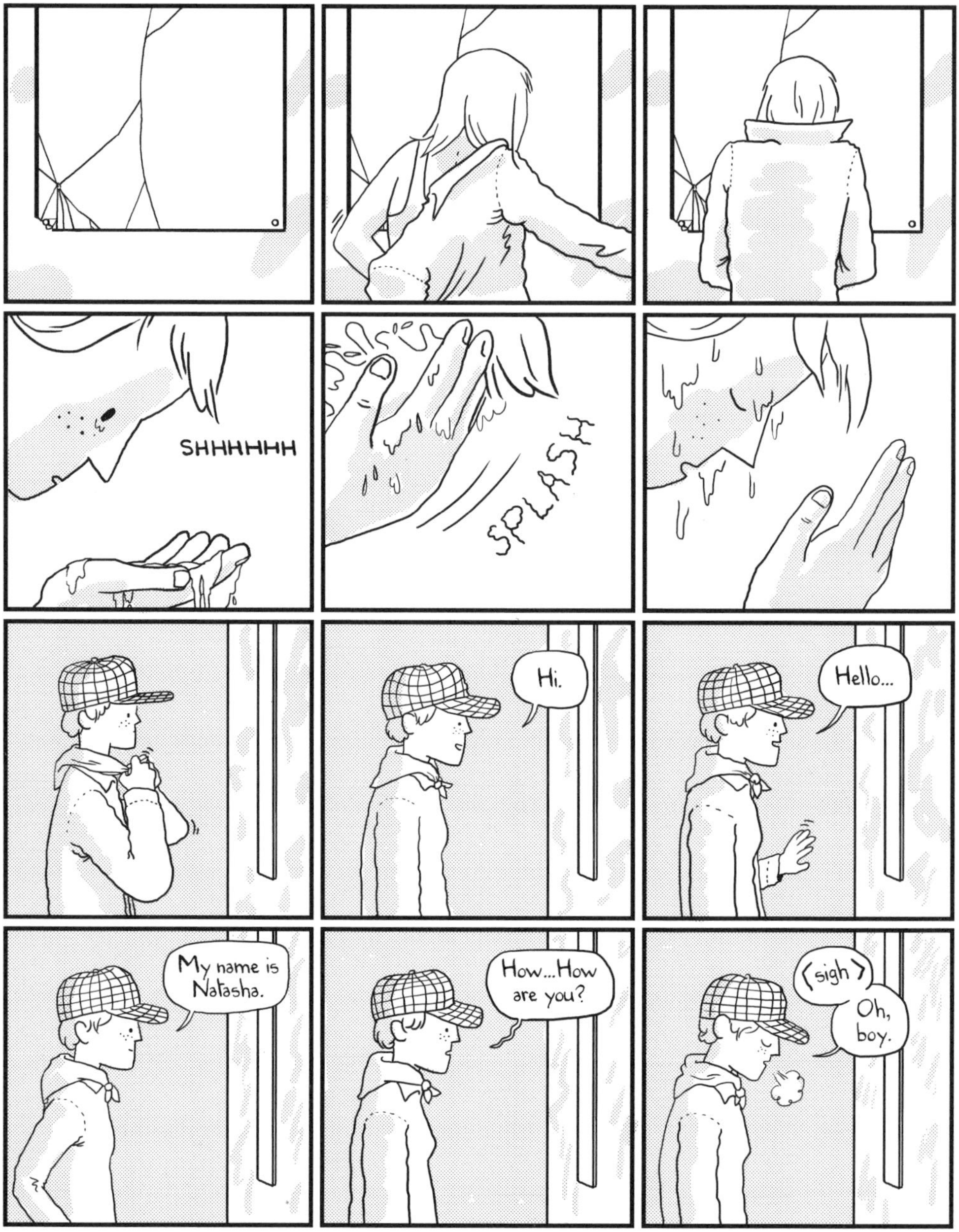
SHHHHHH
SPLASH
Hi.
Hello...
My name is Natasha.
How...How are you?
(sigh)
Oh, boy.

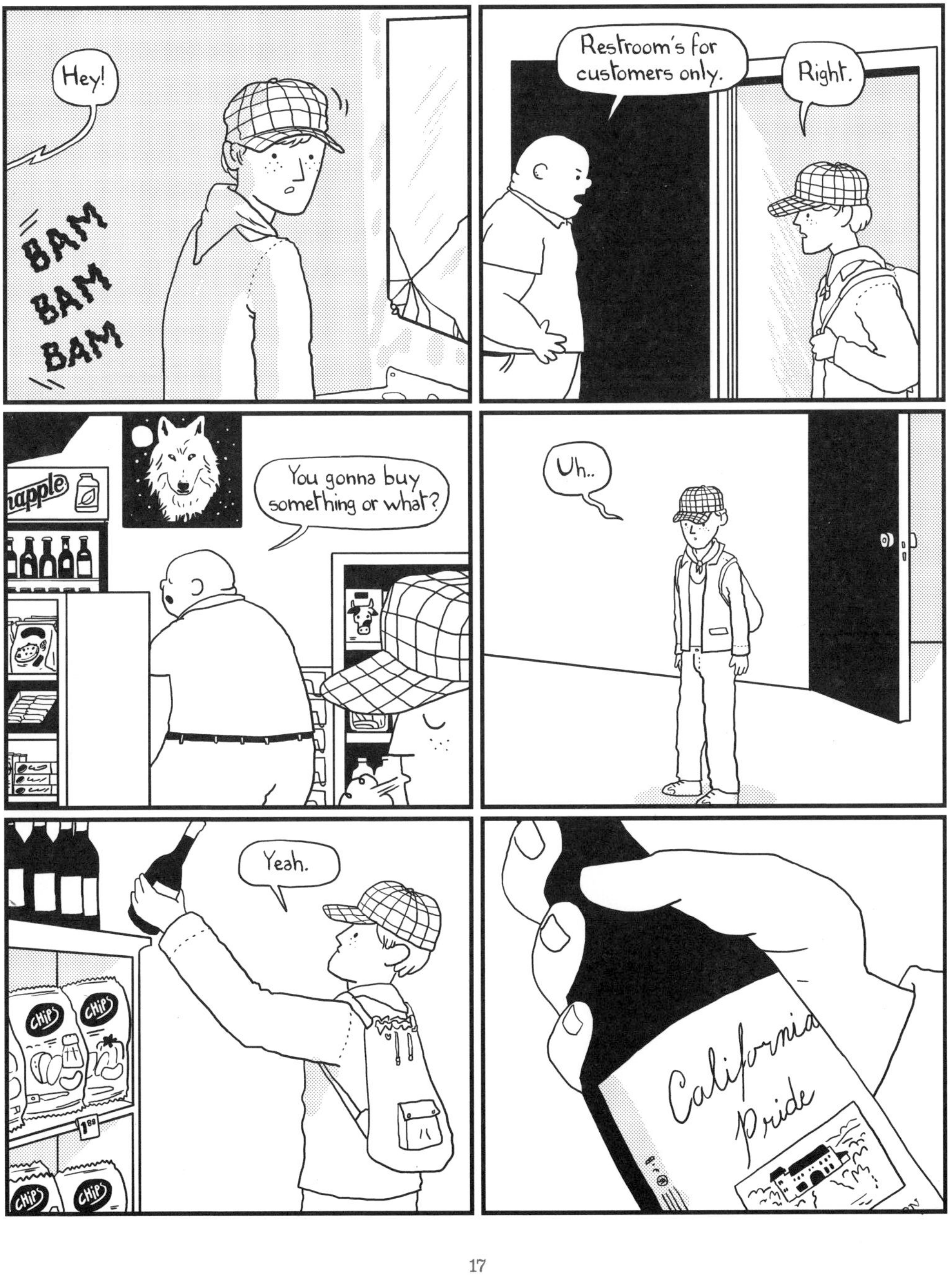
Hey!
BAM
BAM
BAM
Restroom's for customers only.
Right.
You gonna buy something or what?
Uh..
Yeah.
California Pride

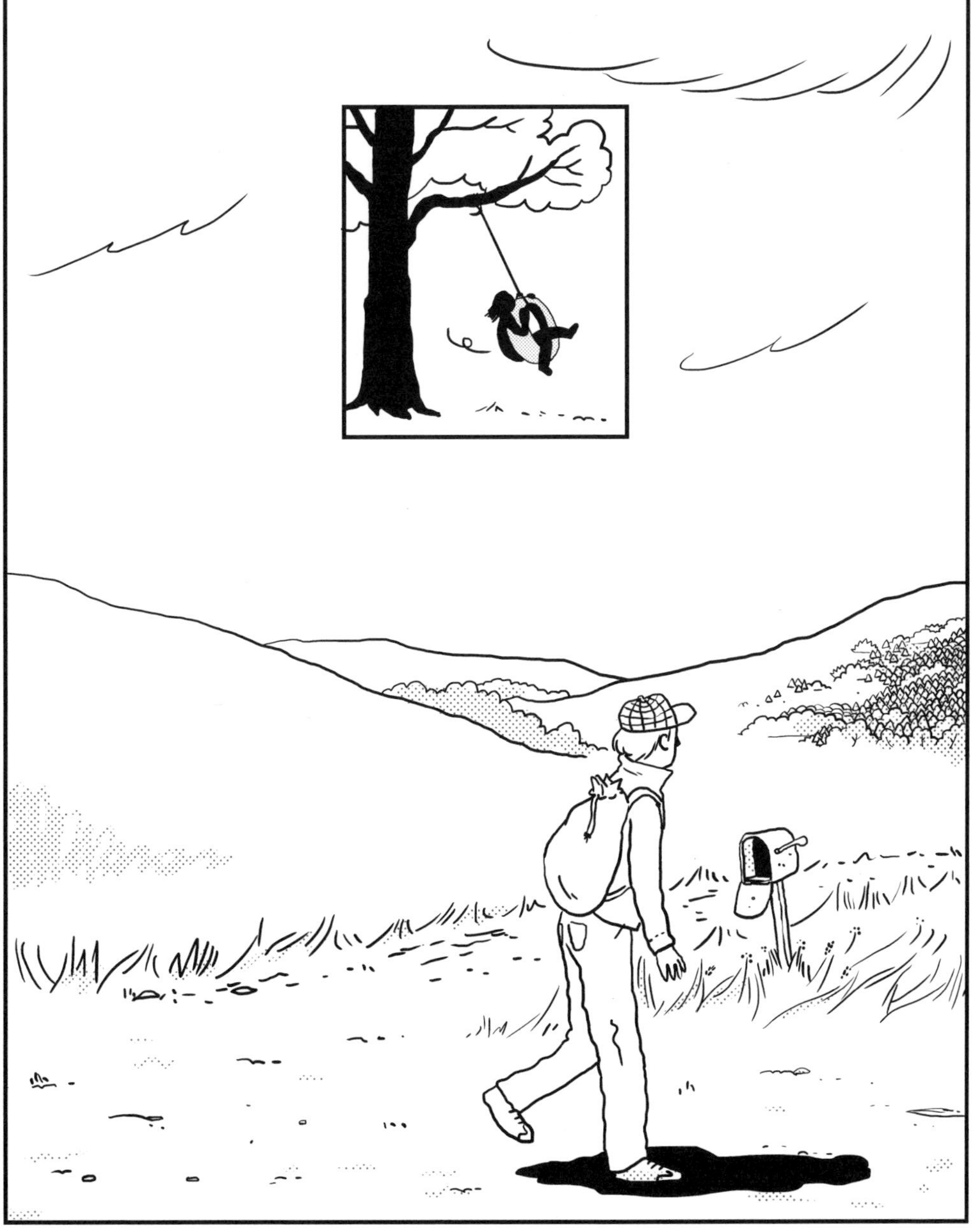

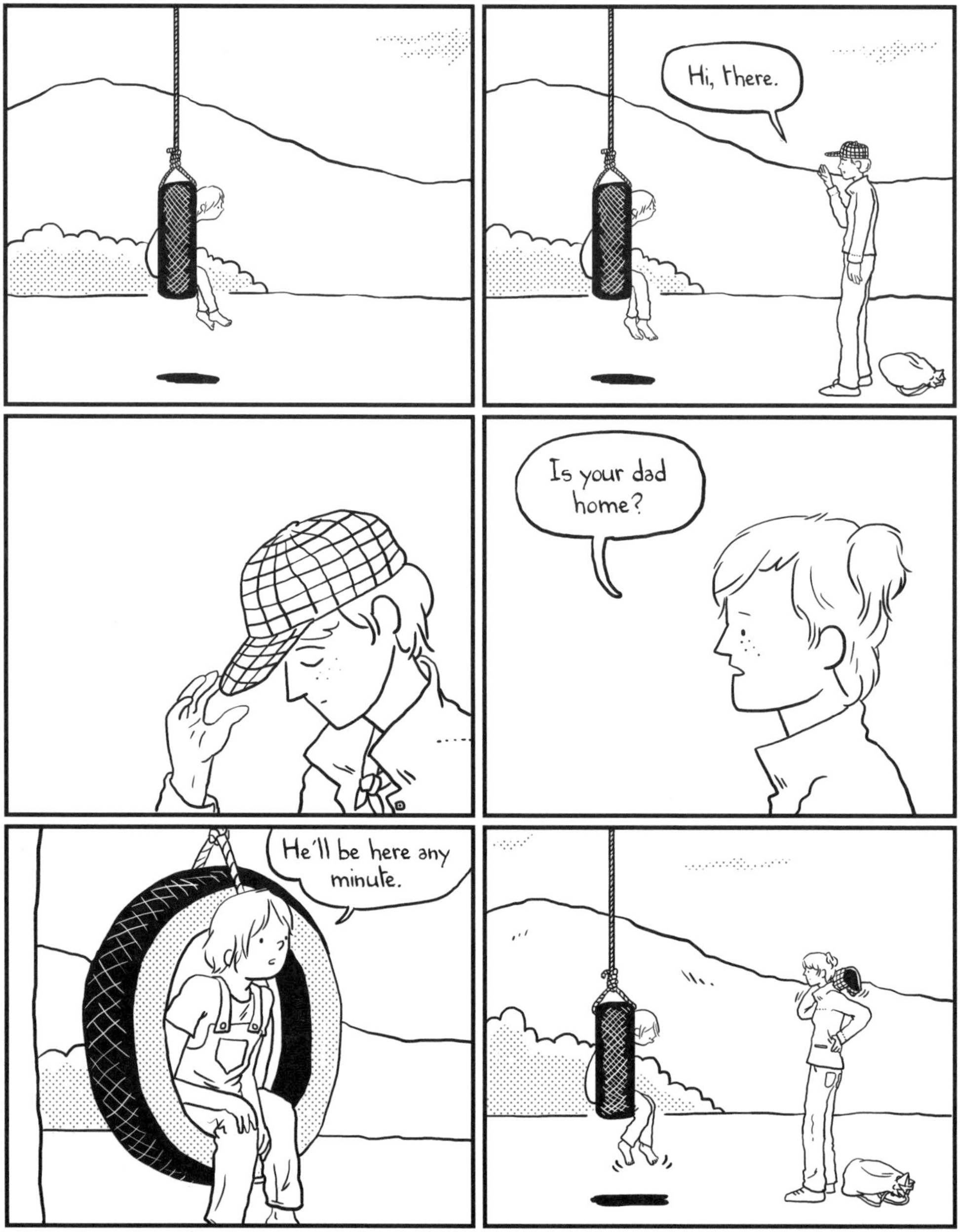
Hi, there.
Is your dad home?
He'll be here any minute.

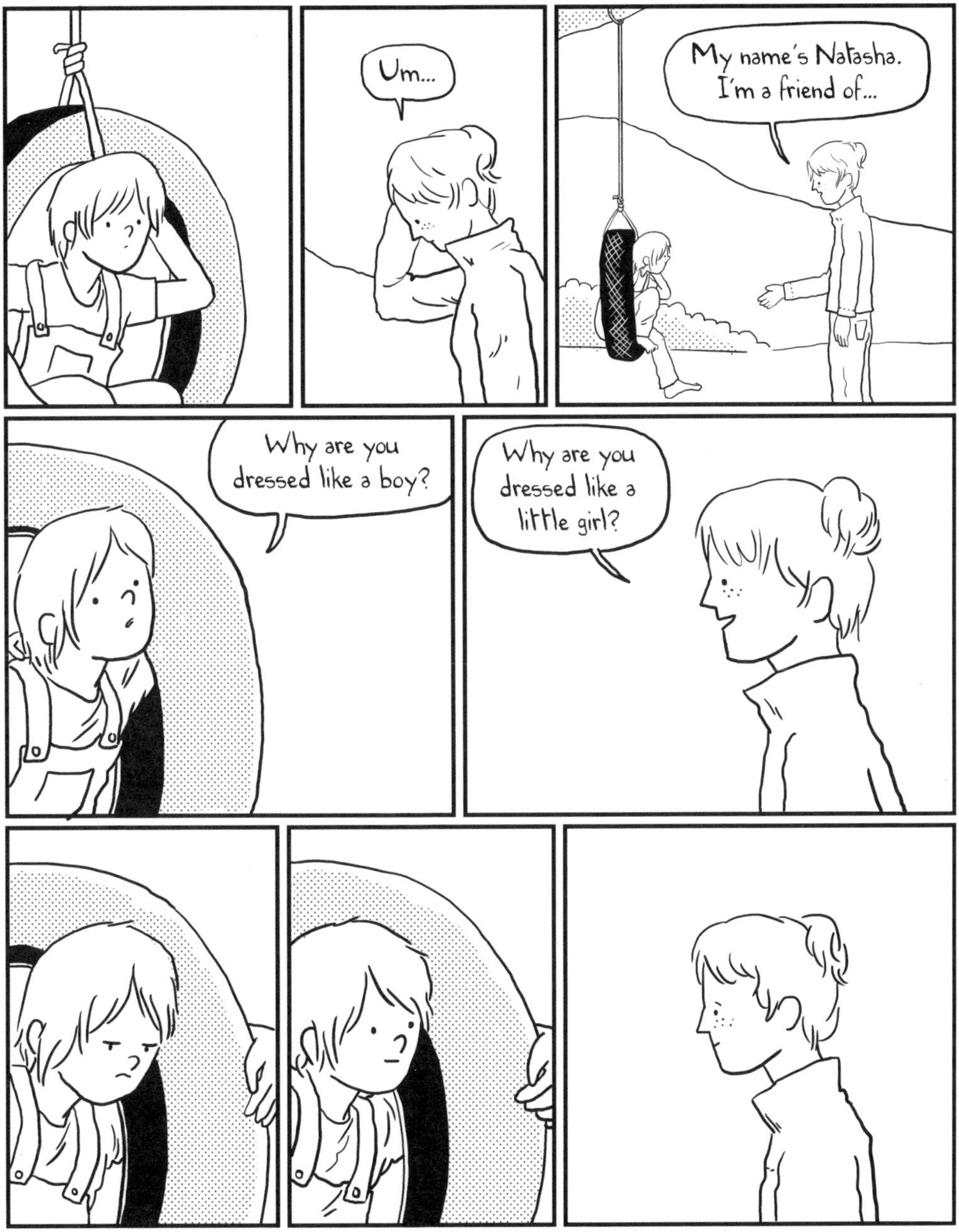

Um...
My name's Natasha. I'm a friend of...
Why are you dressed like a boy?
Why are you dressed like a little girl?

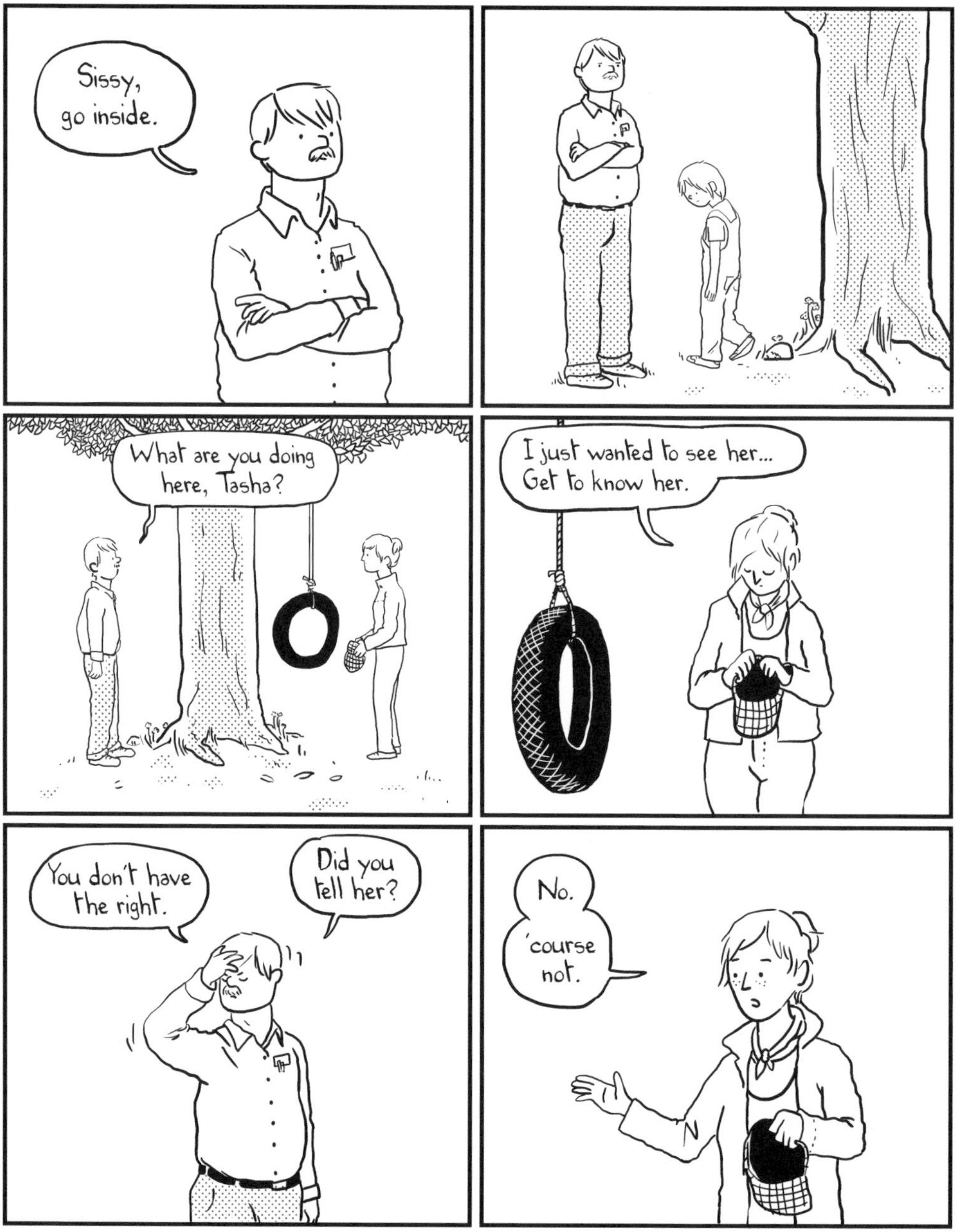
Sissy, go inside.
What are you doing here, Tasha?
I just wanted to see her... Get to know her.
You don't have the right.
Did you tell her?
No.
'course not.

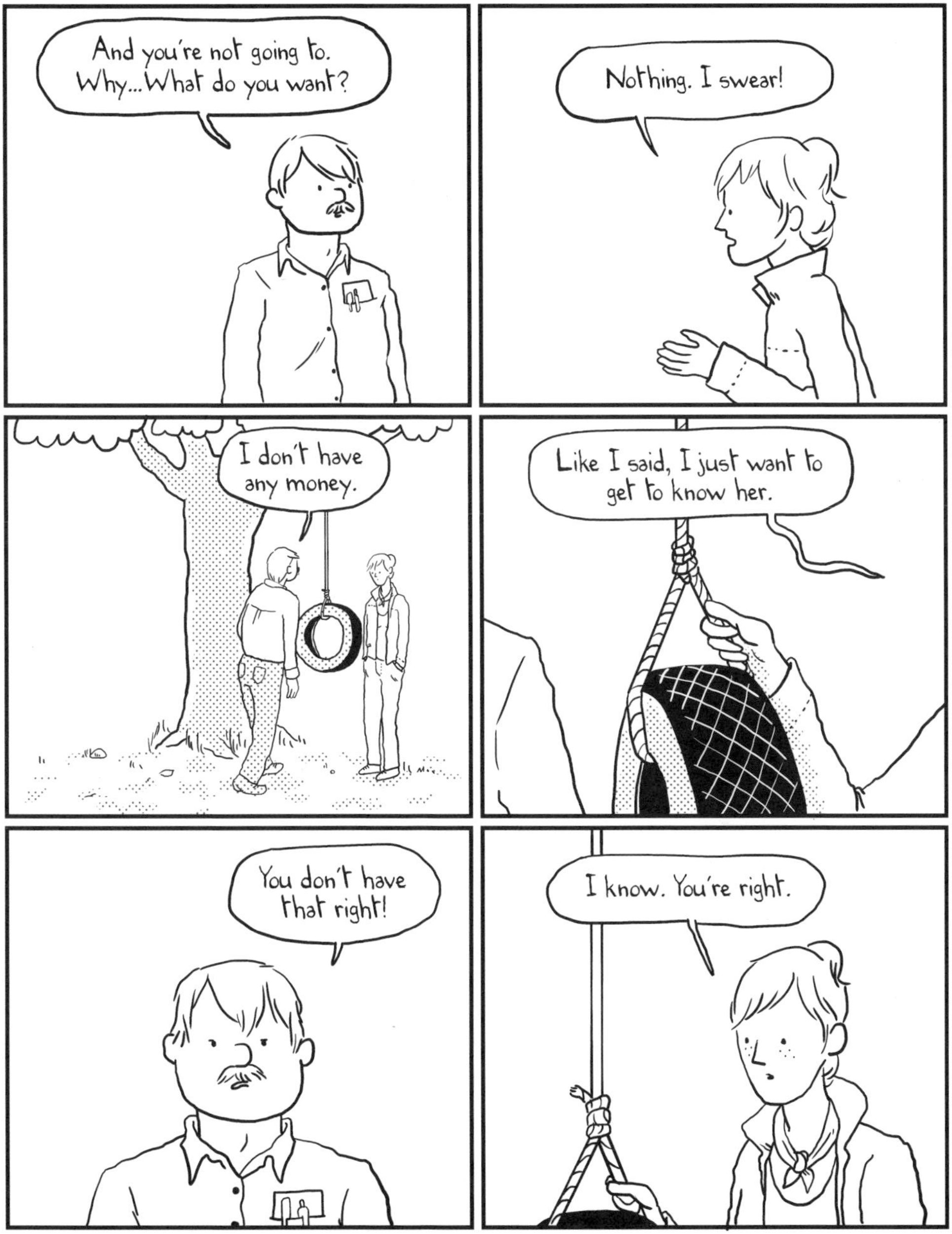
And you're not going to. Why...What do you want?
Nothing. I swear!
I don't have any money.
Like I said, I just want to get to know her.
You don't have that right!
I know. You're right.

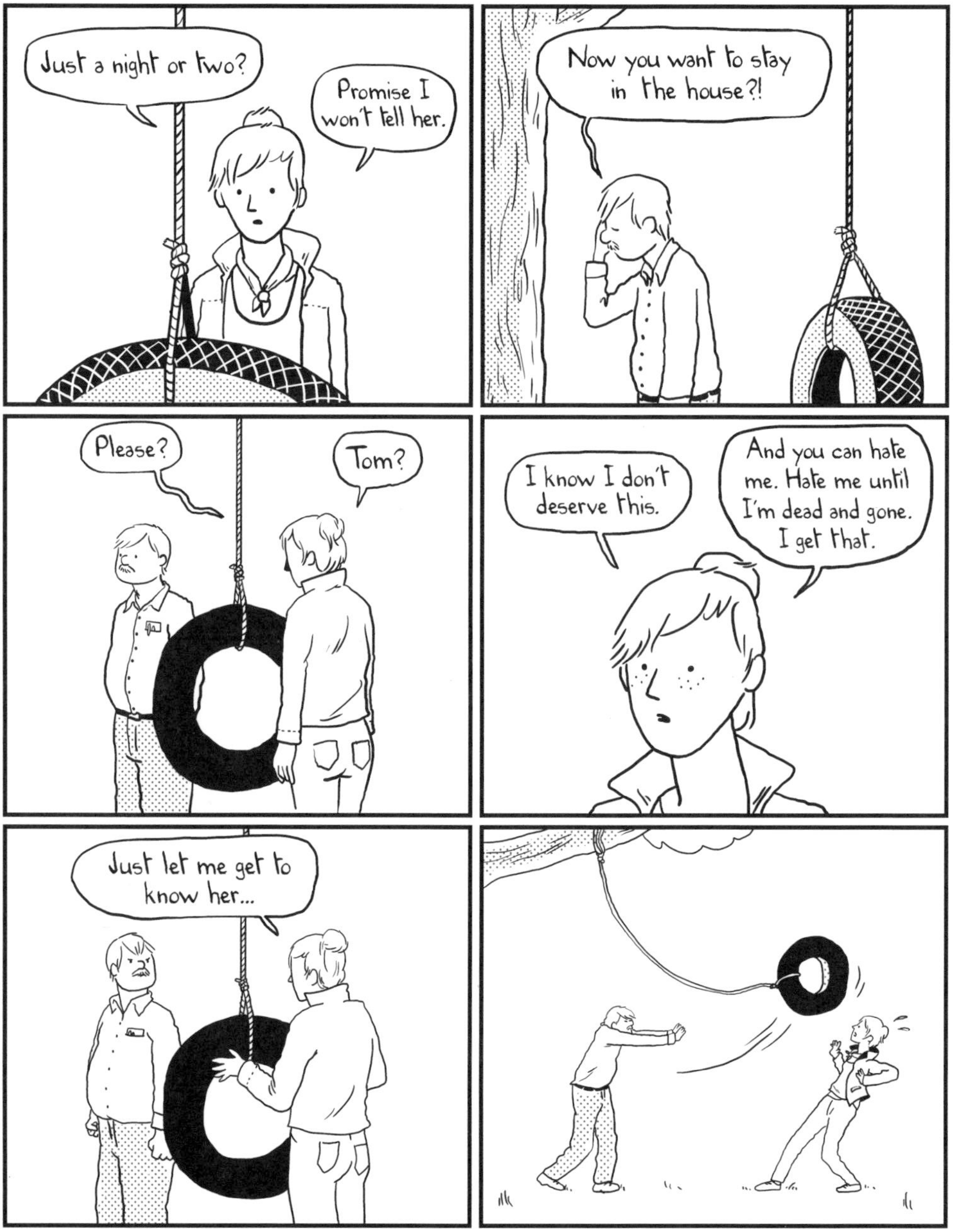
Just a night or two?
Promise I won't tell her.
Now you want to stay in the house?!
Please?
Tom?
I know I don't deserve this.
And you can hate me. Hate me until I'm dead and gone. I get that.
Just let me get to know her...

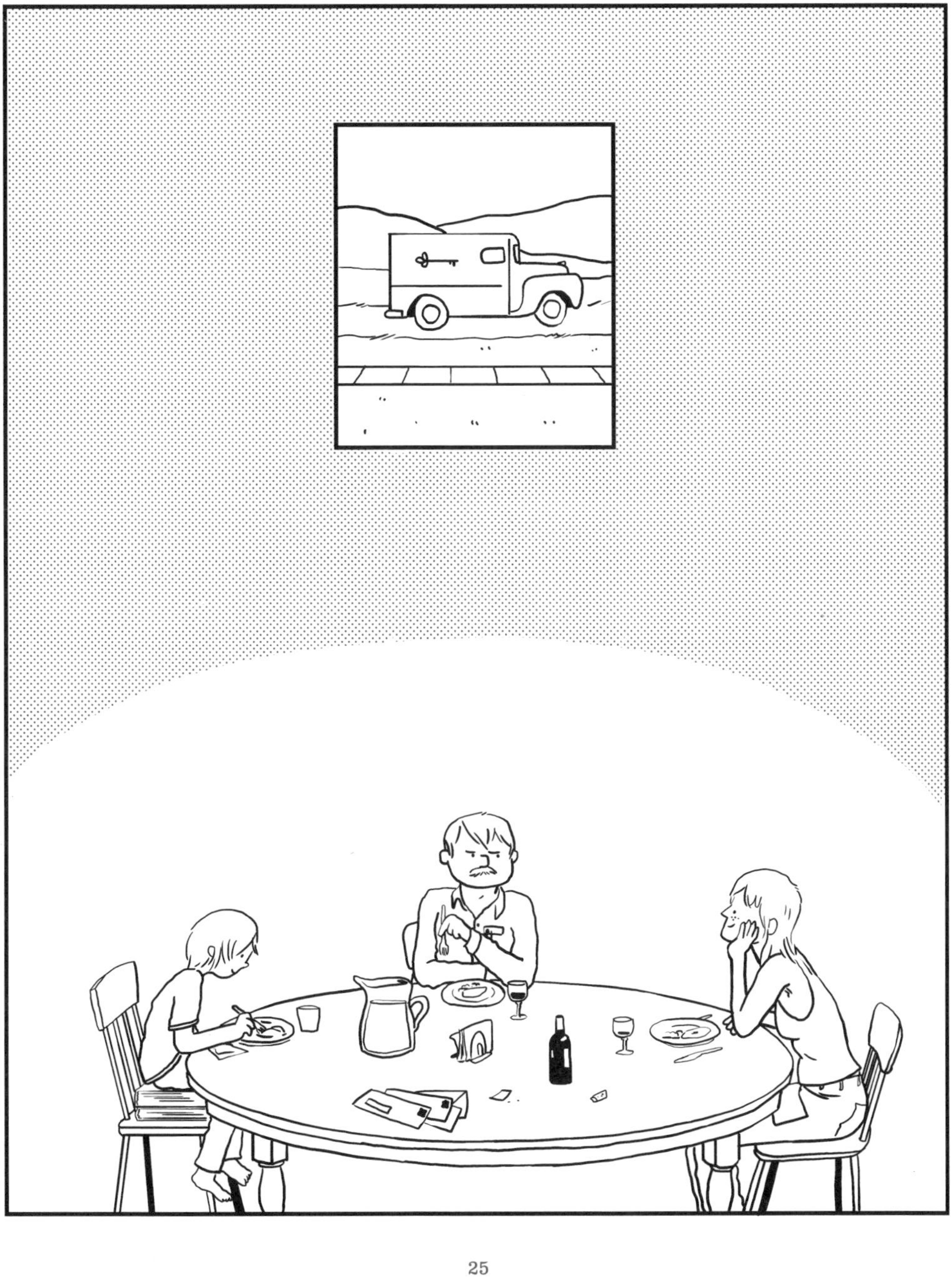

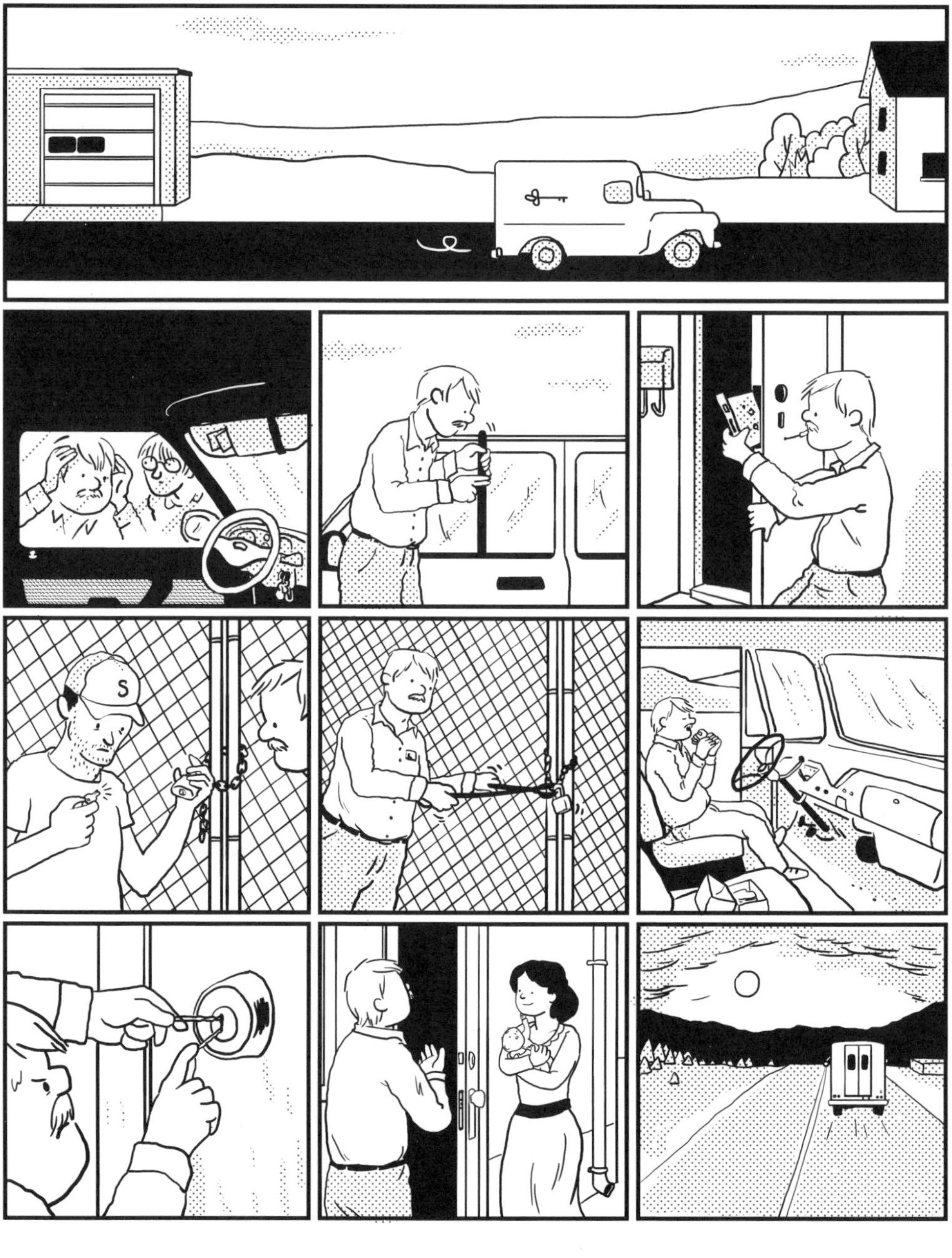

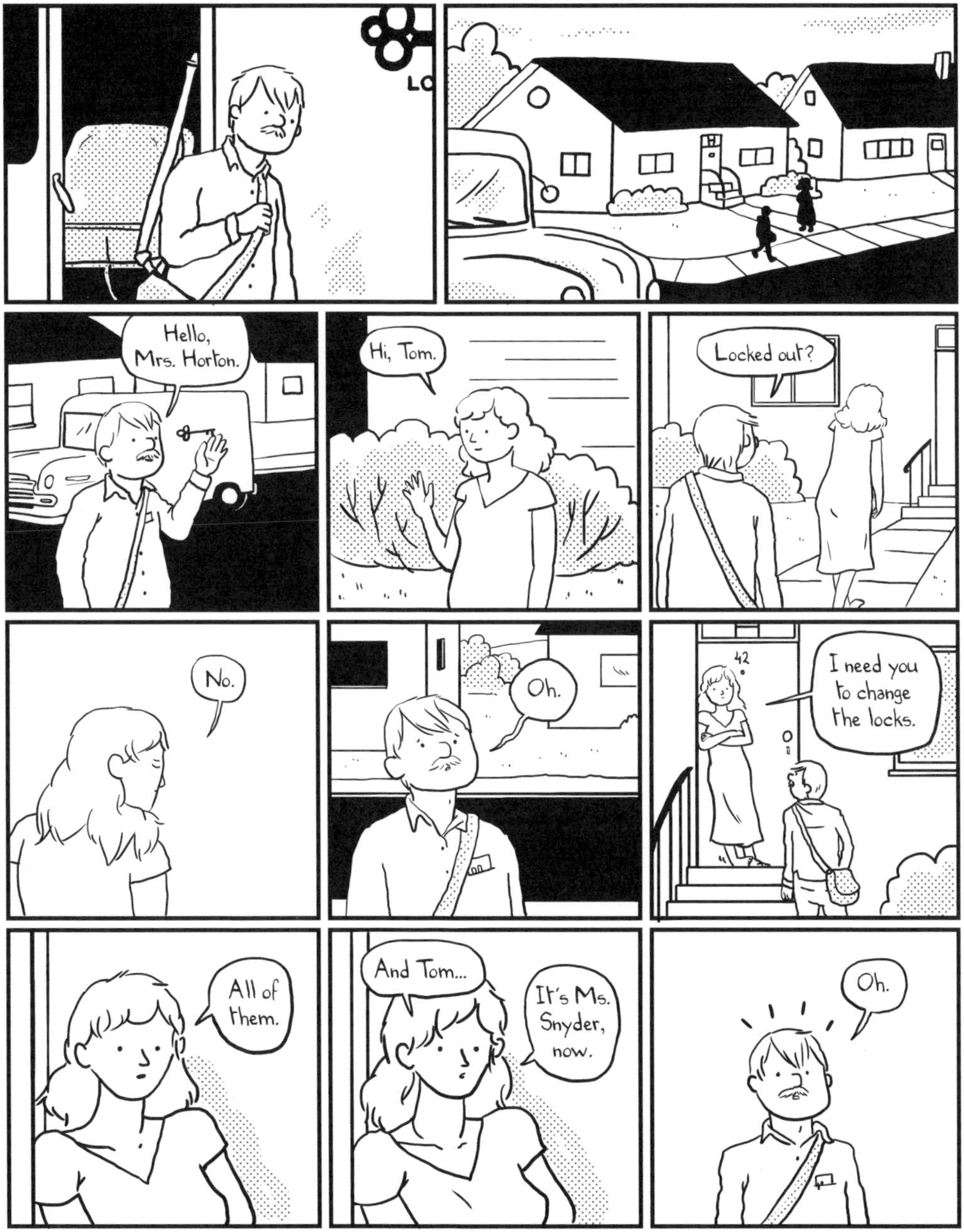
LO
Hello, Mrs. Horton.
Hi, Tom.
Locked out?
No.
Oh.
42
I need you to change the locks.
All of them.
And Tom...
It's Ms. Snyder, now.
Oh.

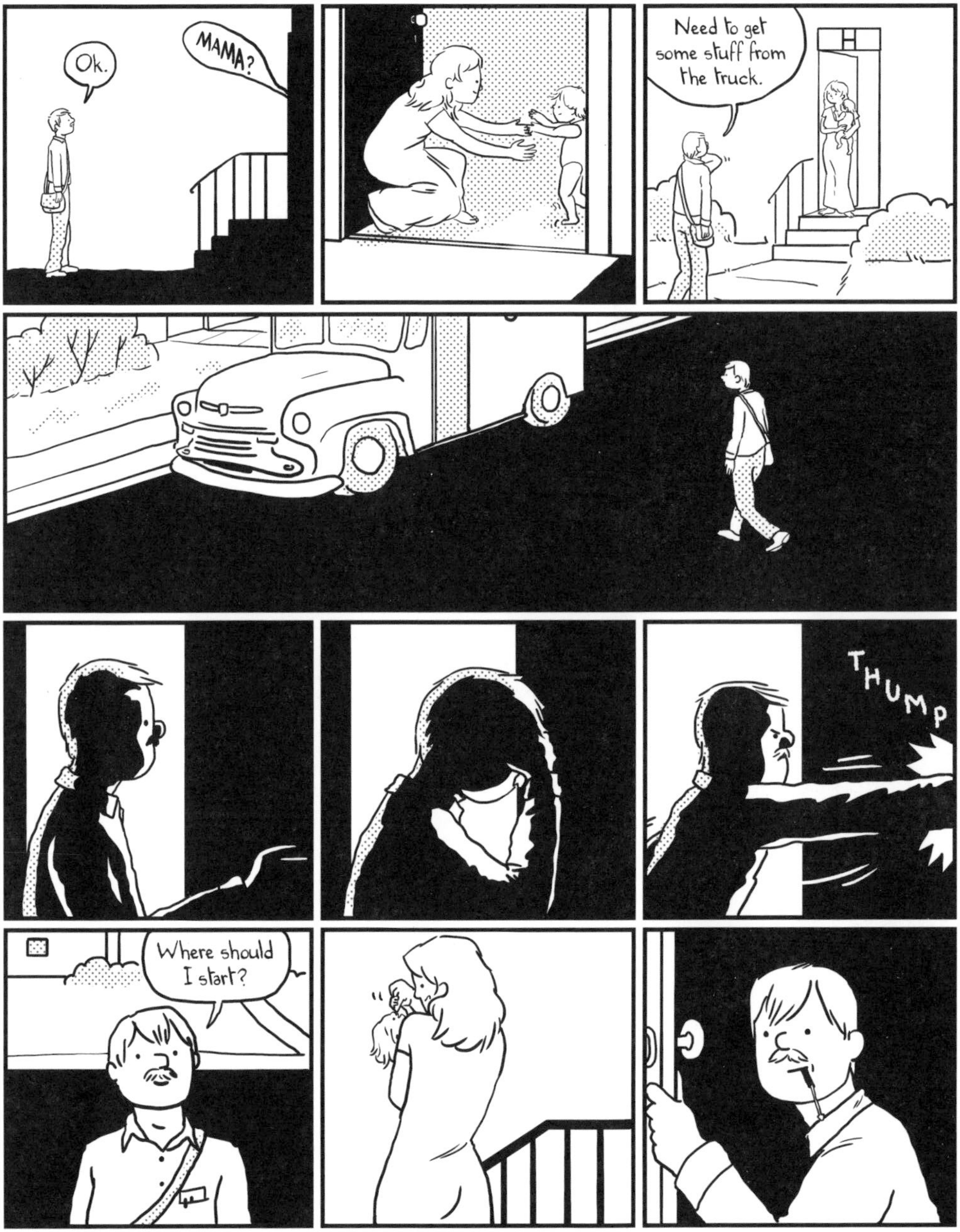
Ok.
MAMA?
Need to get some stuff from the truck.
THUMP
Where should I start?

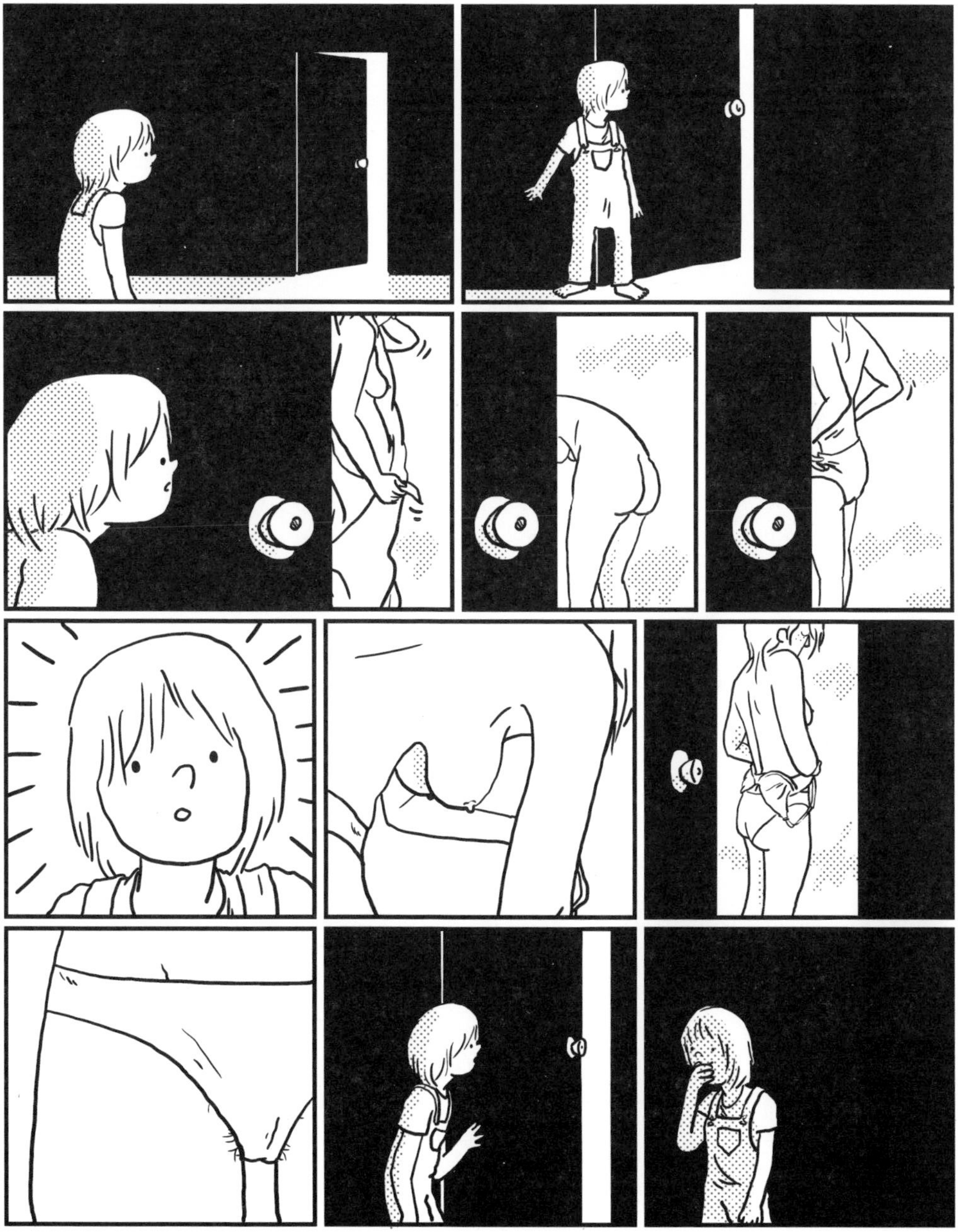

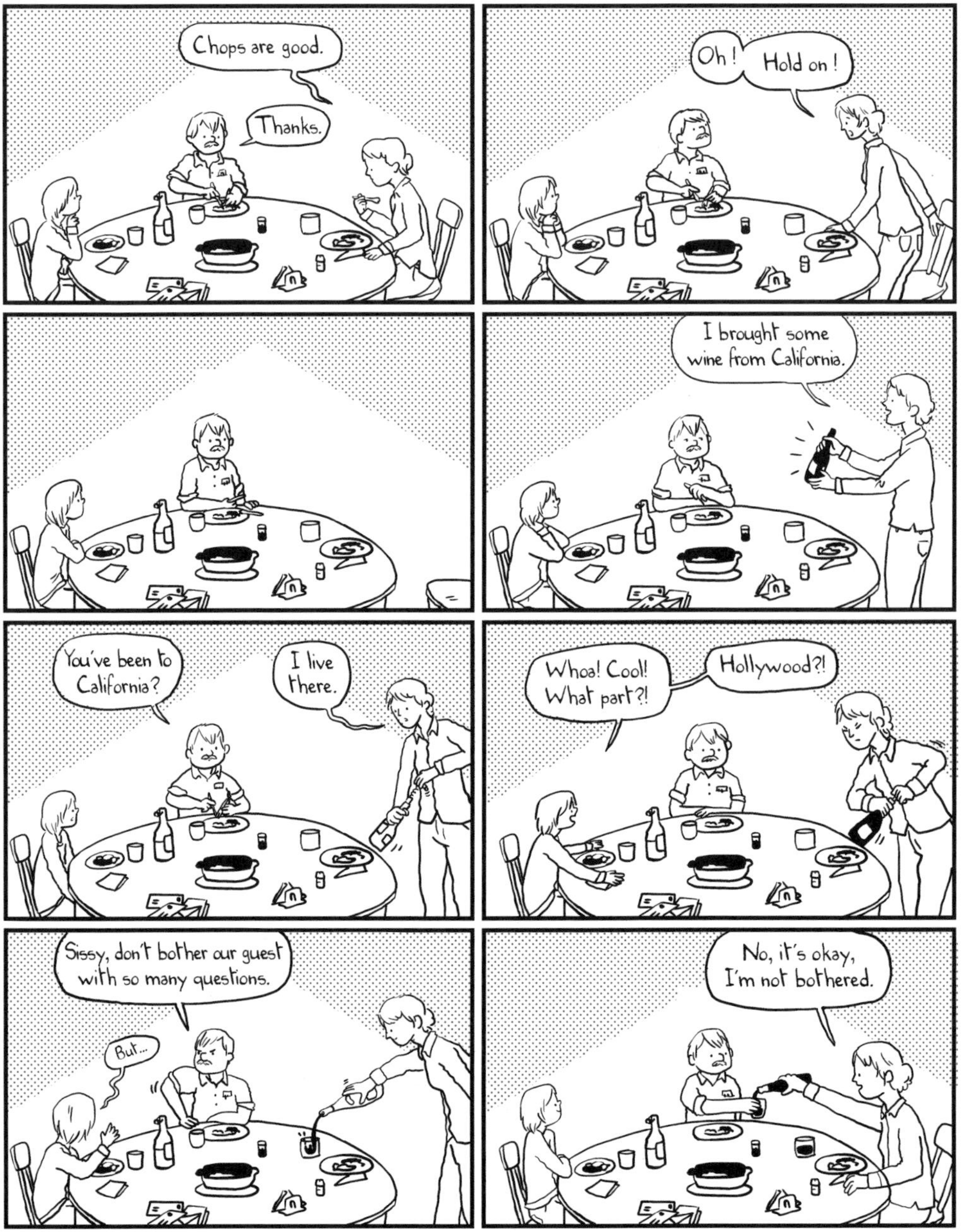
Chops are good.
Thanks.
Oh!
Hold on!
I brought some wine from California.
You've been to California?
I live there.
Whoa! Cool! What part?!
Hollywood?!
Sissy, don't bother our guest with so many questions.
But...
No, it's okay, I'm not bothered.

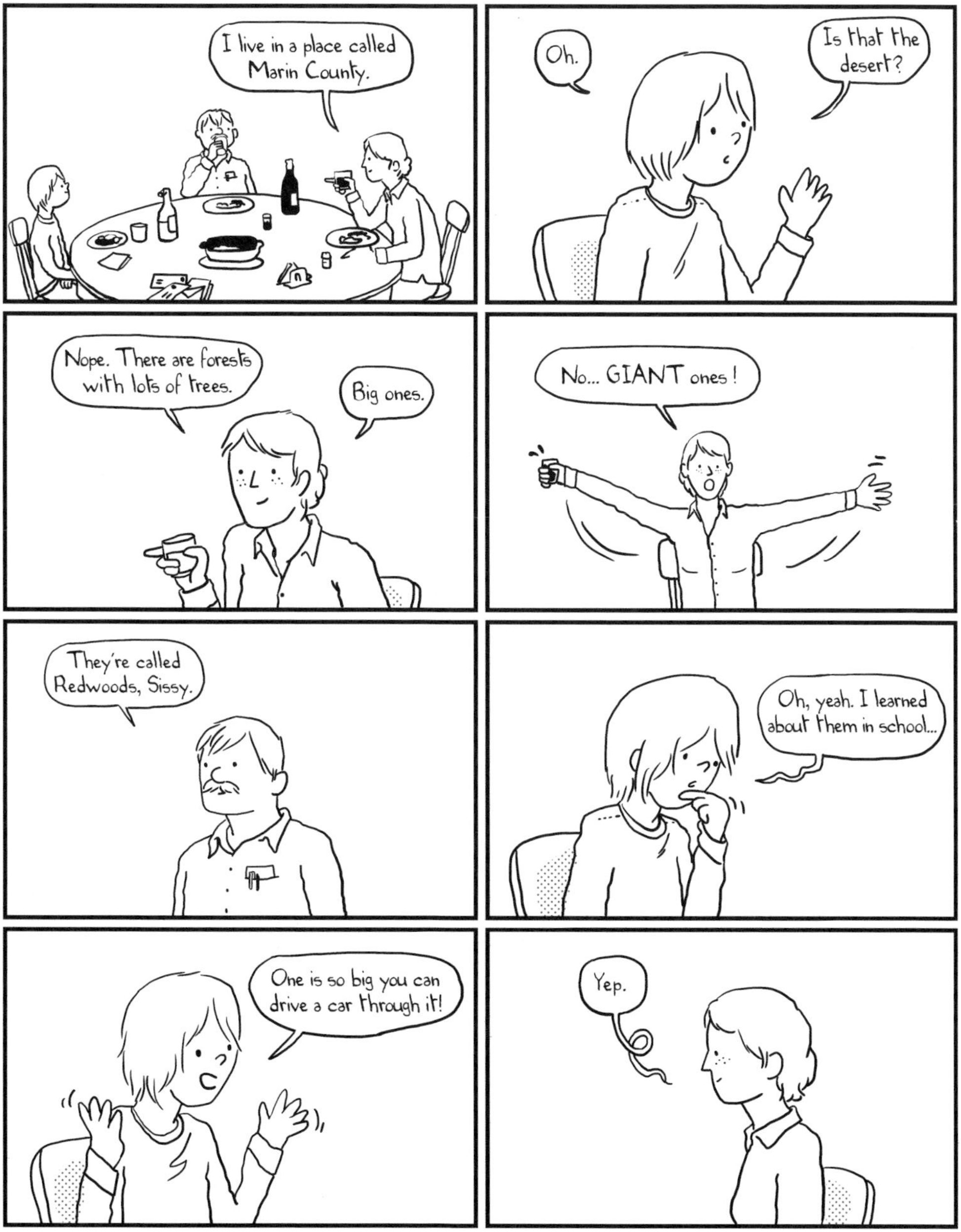
I live in a place called Marin County.
Oh.
Is that the desert?
Nope. There are forests with lots of trees.
Big ones.
No... GIANT ones!
They're called Redwoods, Sissy.
Oh, yeah. I learned about them in school...
One is so big you can drive a car through it!
Yep.

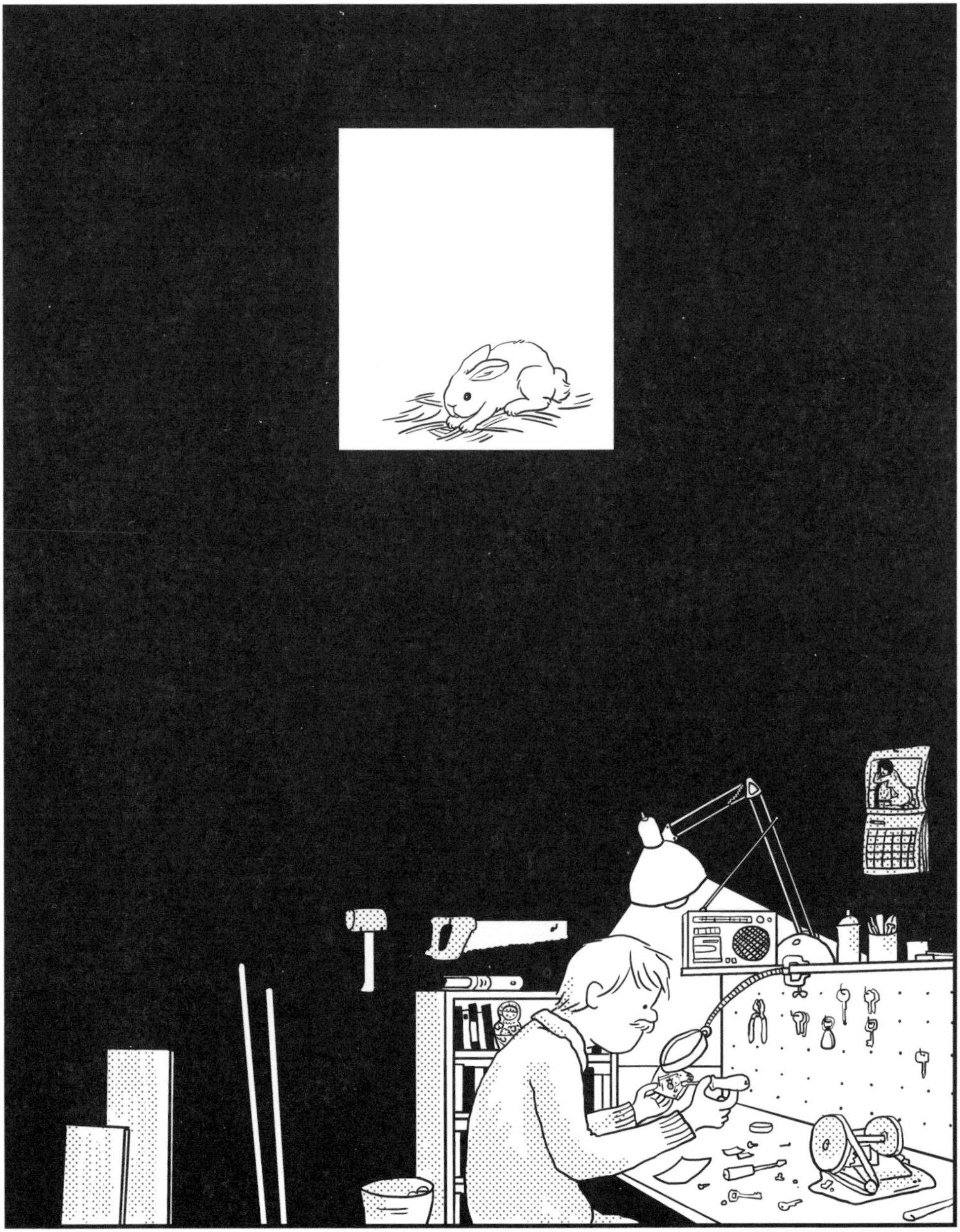

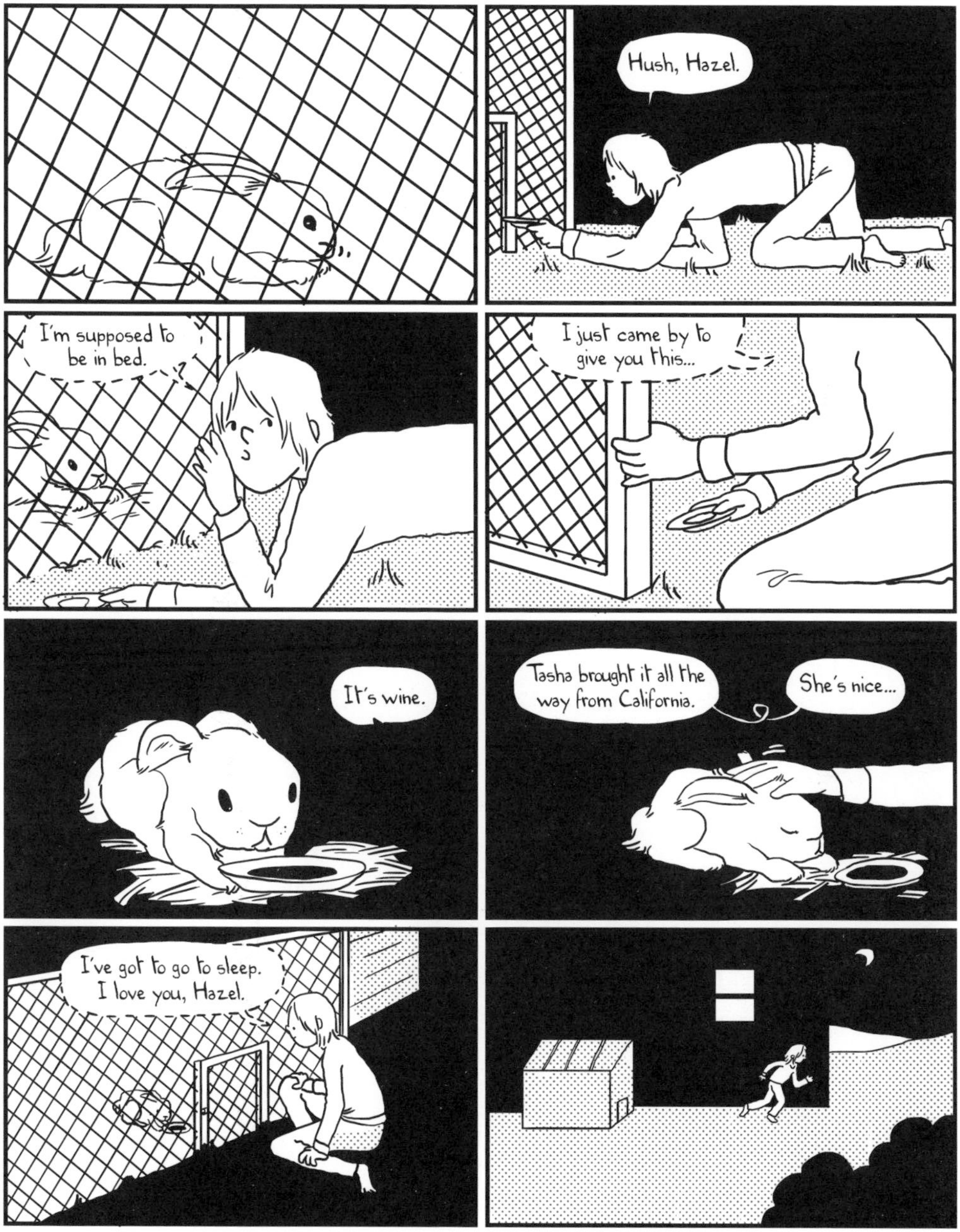
Hush, Hazel.
I'm supposed to be in bed.
I just came by to give you this...
It's wine.
Tasha brought it all the way from California.
She's nice...
I've got to go to sleep. I love you, Hazel.

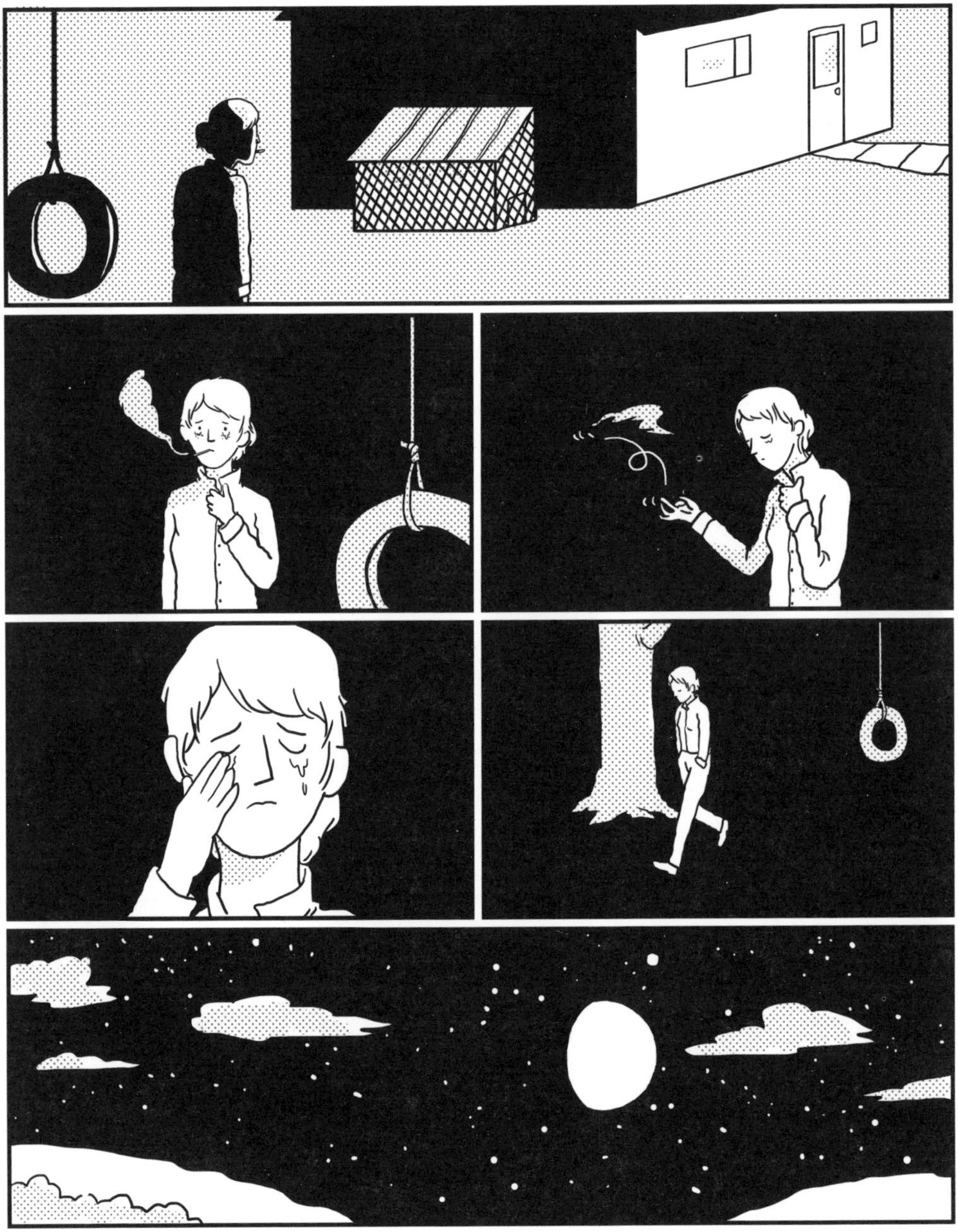

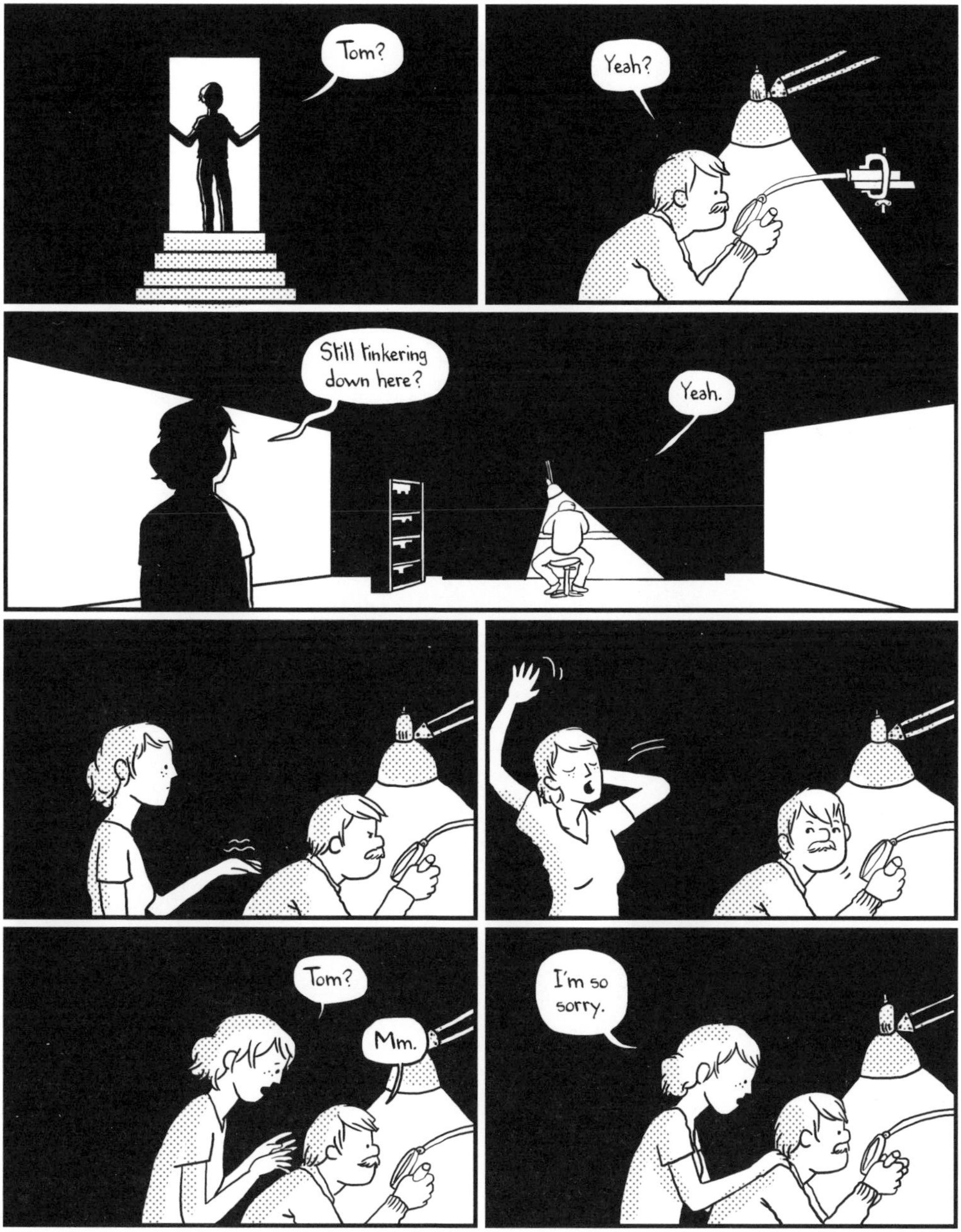
Tom?
Yeah?
Still tinkering down here?
Yeah.
Tom?
Mm.
I'm so sorry.

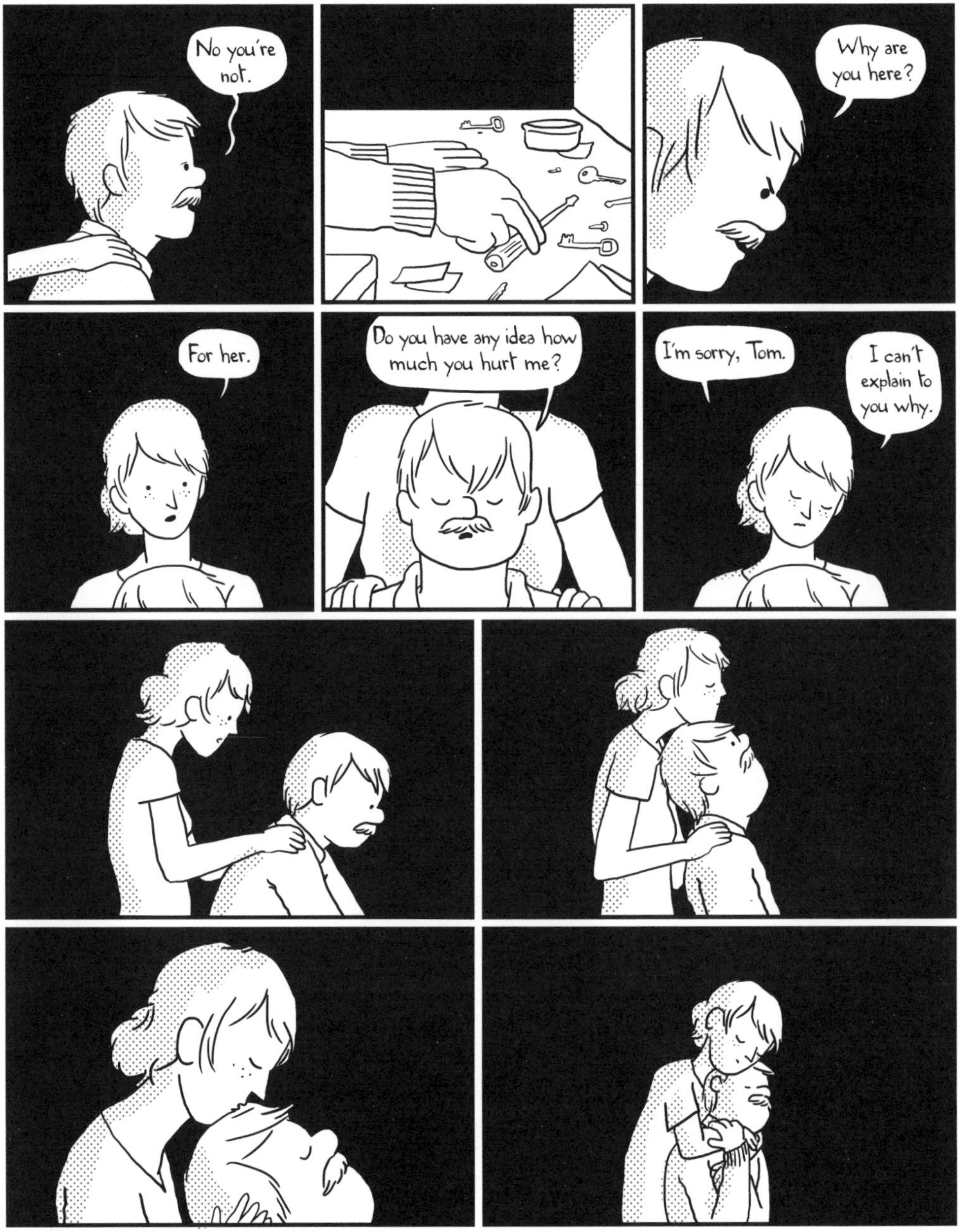
No you're not.
Why are you here?
For her.
Do you have any idea how much you hurt me?
I'm sorry, Tom.
I can't explain to you why.

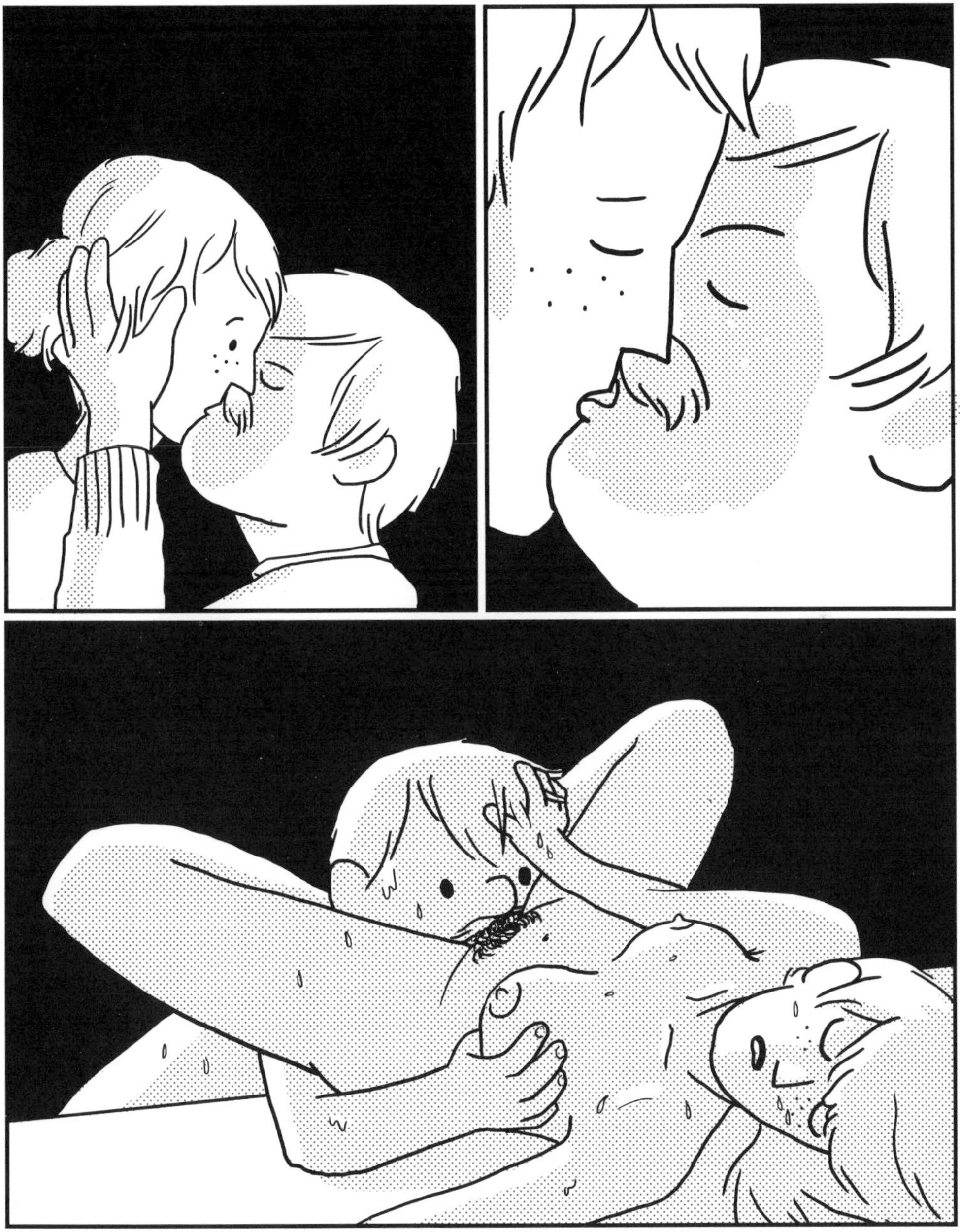

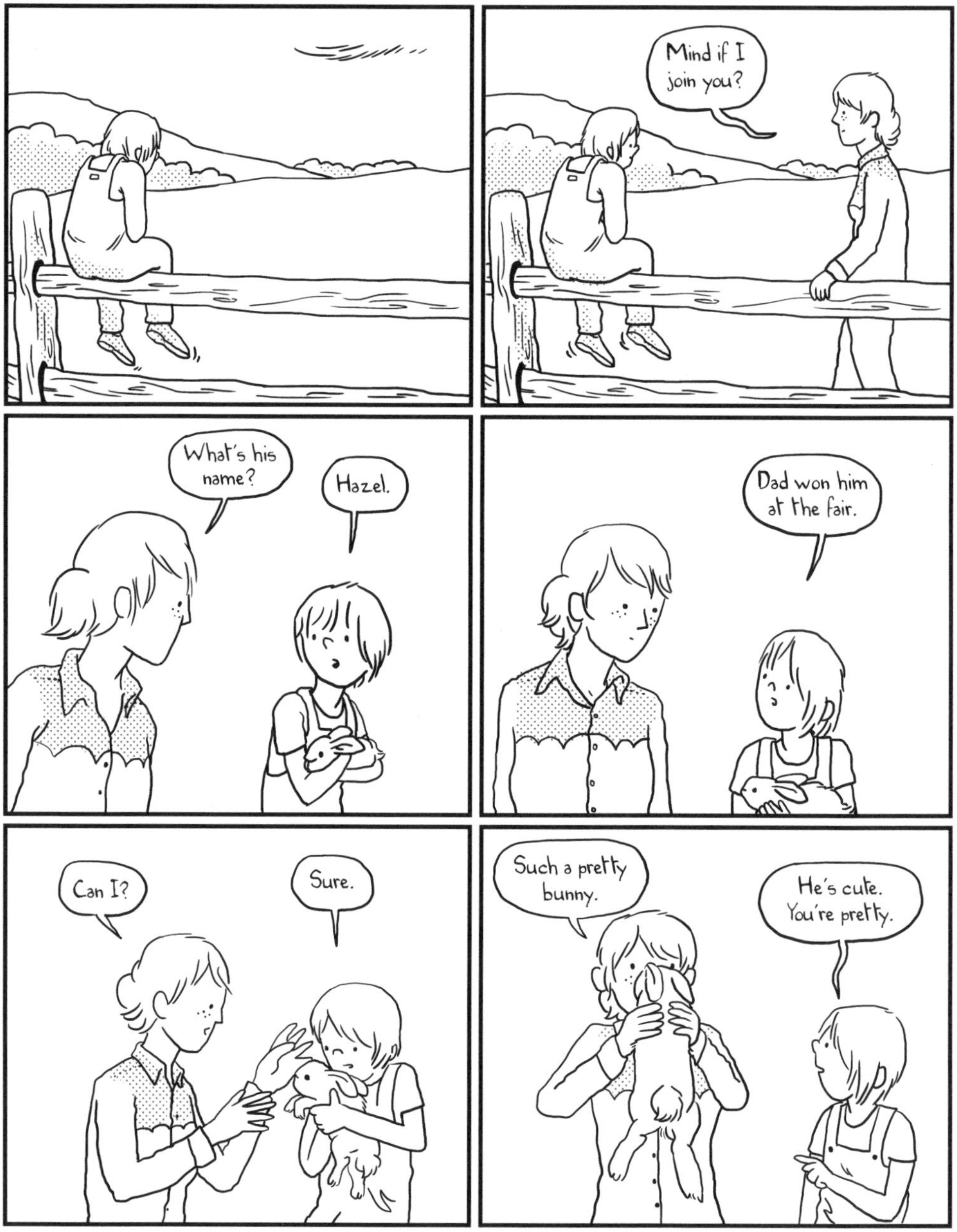
Mind if I join you?
What's his name?
Hazel.
Dad won him at the fair.
Can I?
Sure.
Such a pretty bunny.
He's cute. You're pretty.

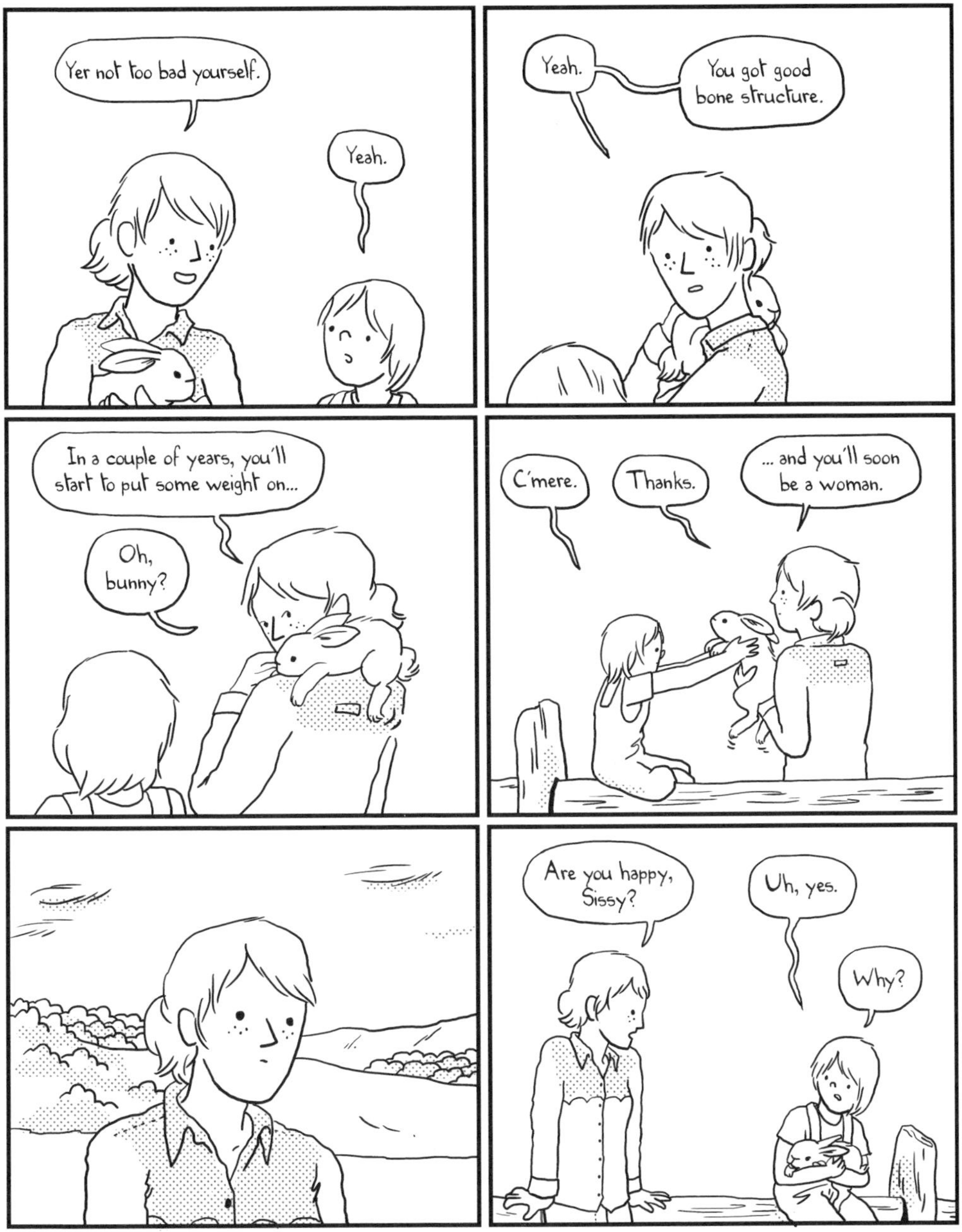
Yer not too bad yourself.
Yeah.
Yeah.
You got good bone structure.
In a couple of years, you'll start to put some weight on...
Oh, bunny?
C'mere.
Thanks.
... and you'll soon be a woman.
Are you happy, Sissy?
Uh, yes.
Why?

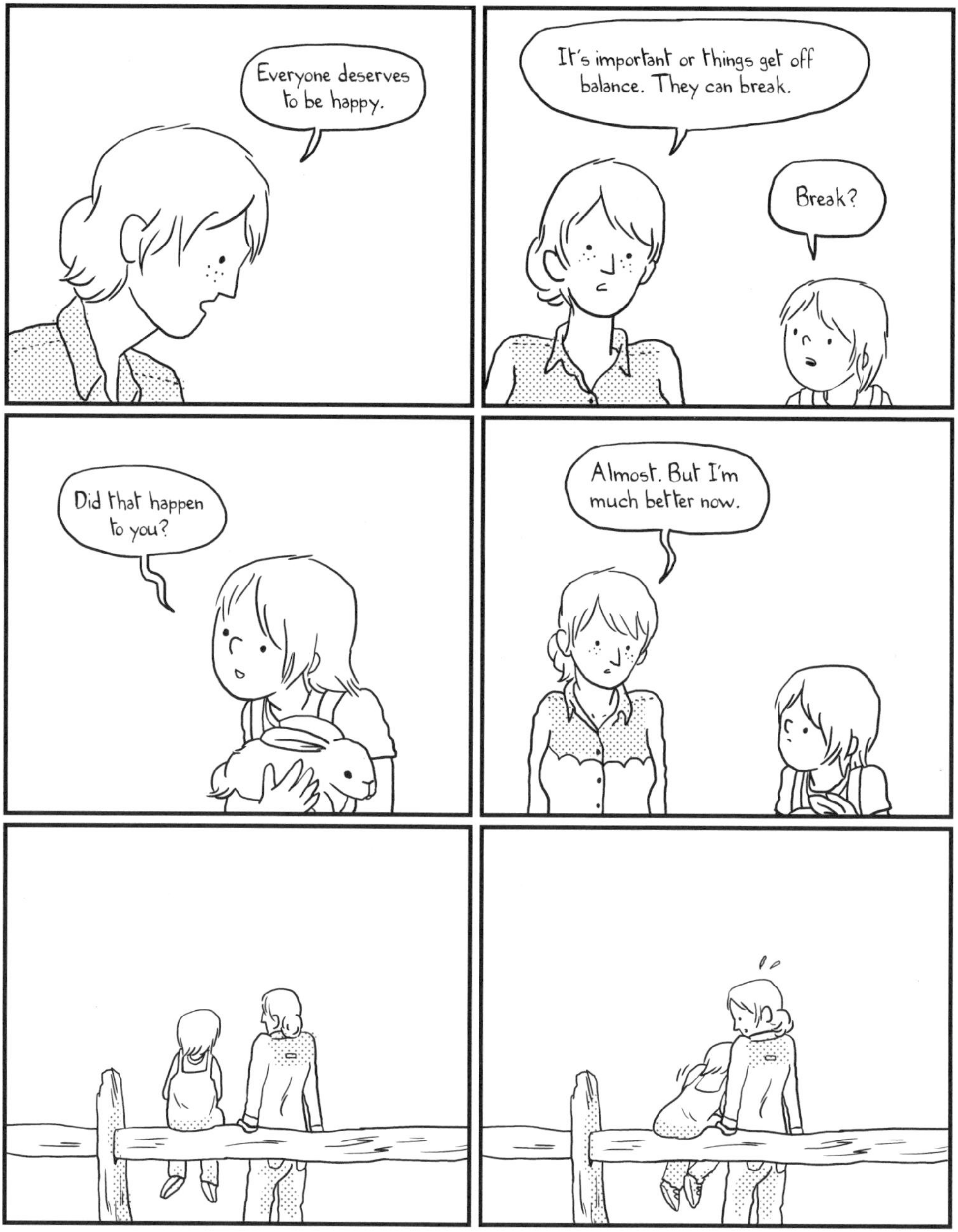
Everyone deserves to be happy.
It's important or things get off balance. They can break.
Break?
Did that happen to you?
Almost. But I'm much better now.

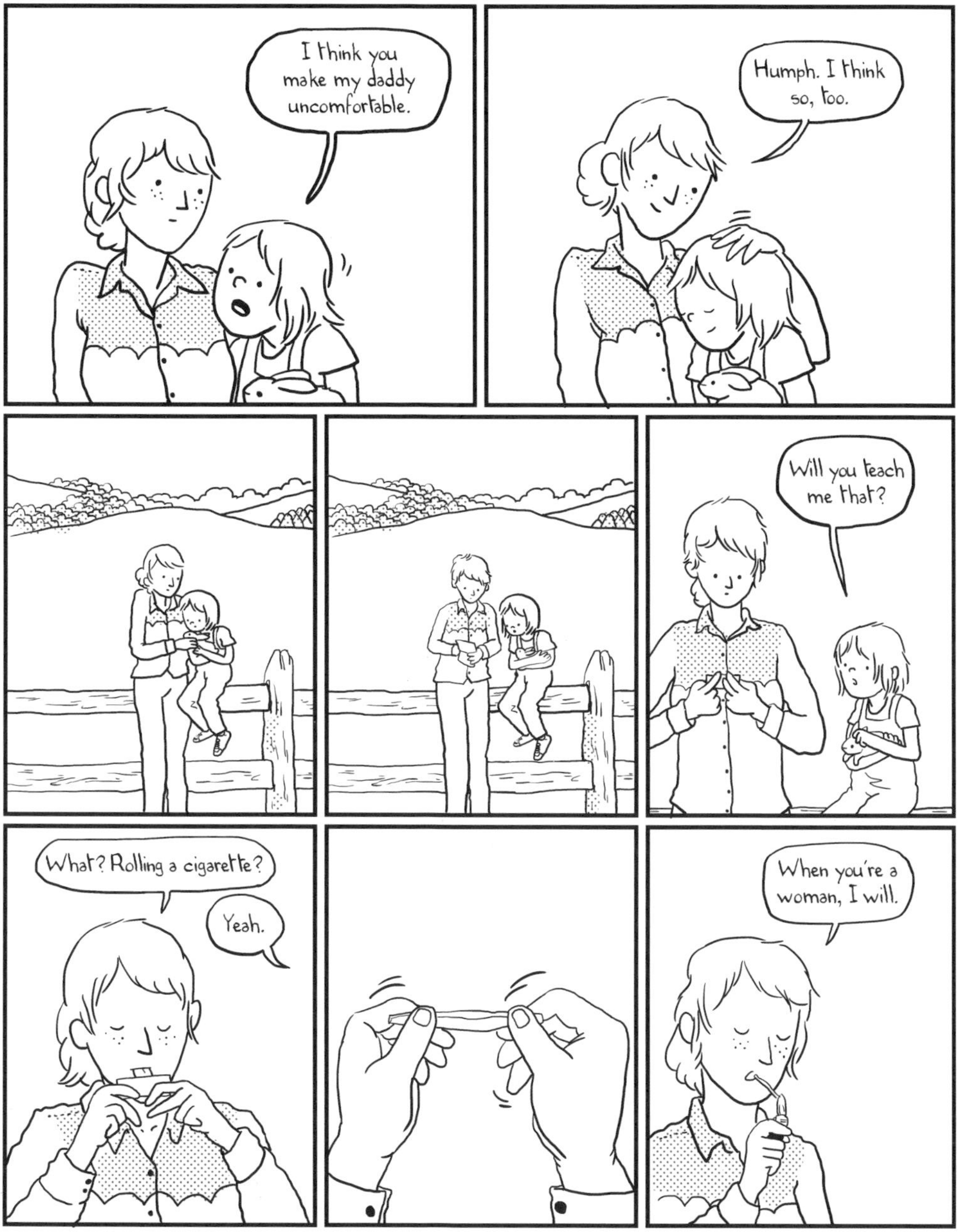
I think you make my daddy uncomfortable.
Humph. I think so, too.
Will you teach me that?
What? Rolling a cigarette?
Yeah.
When you're a woman, I will.

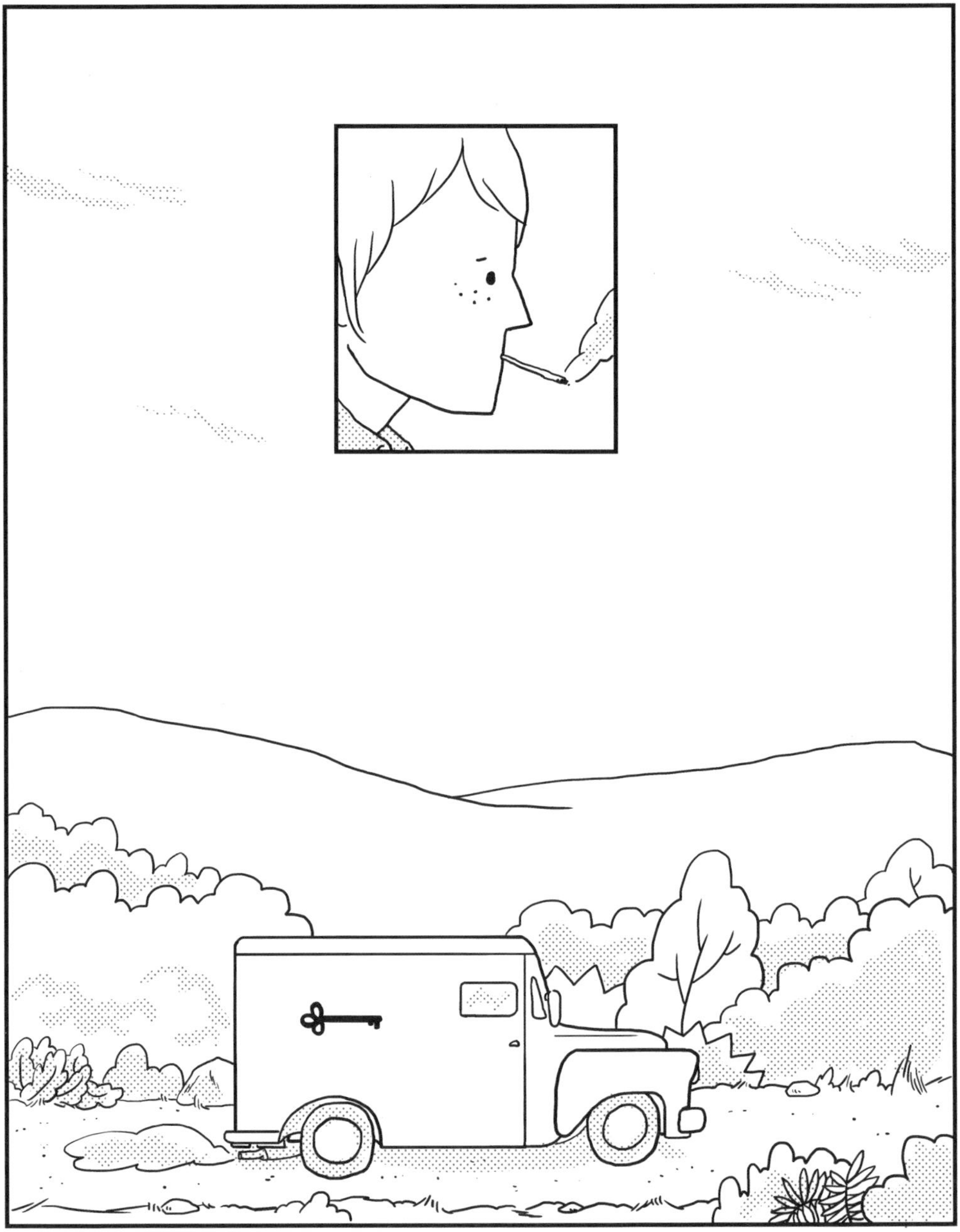

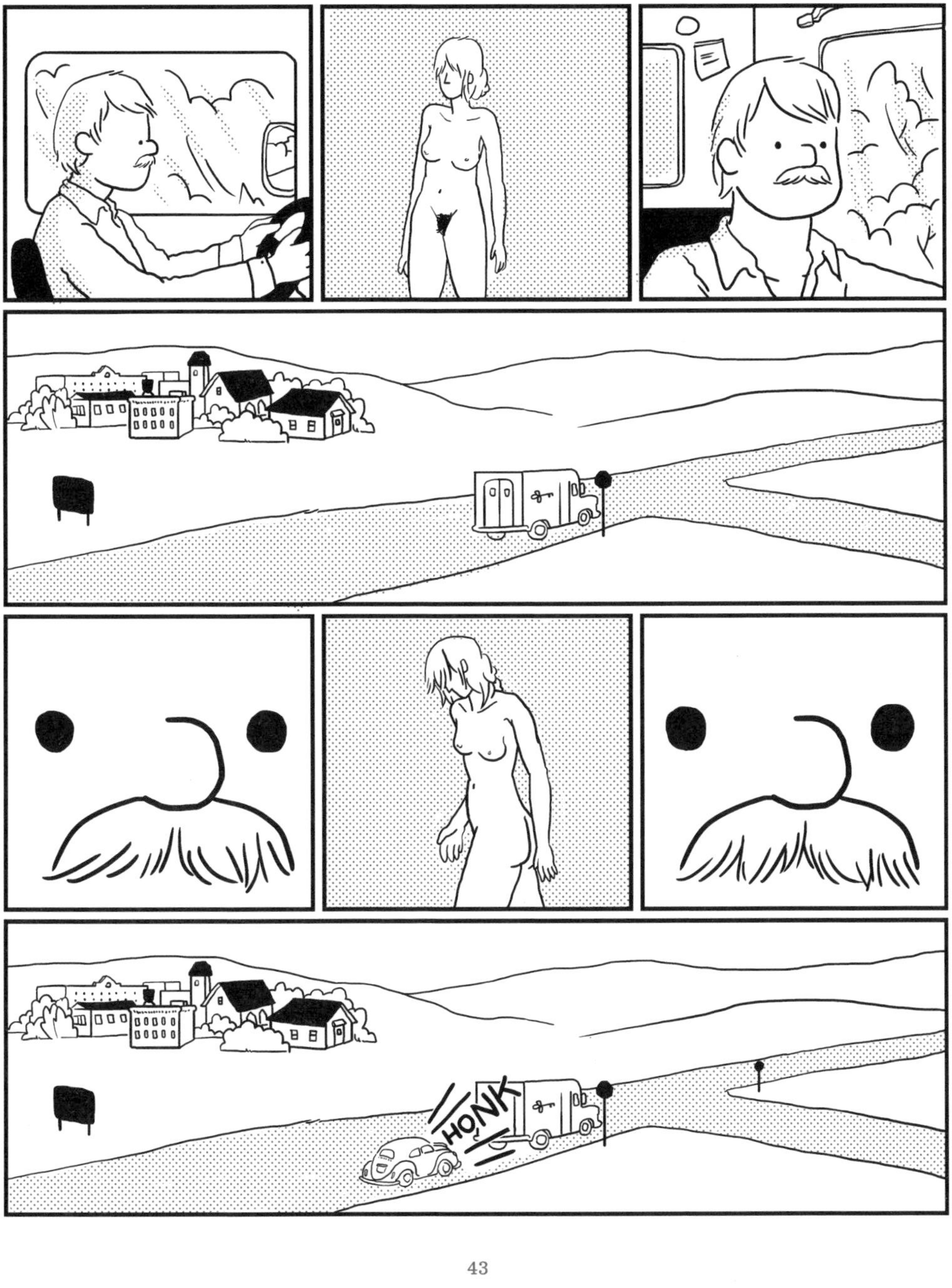
HONK

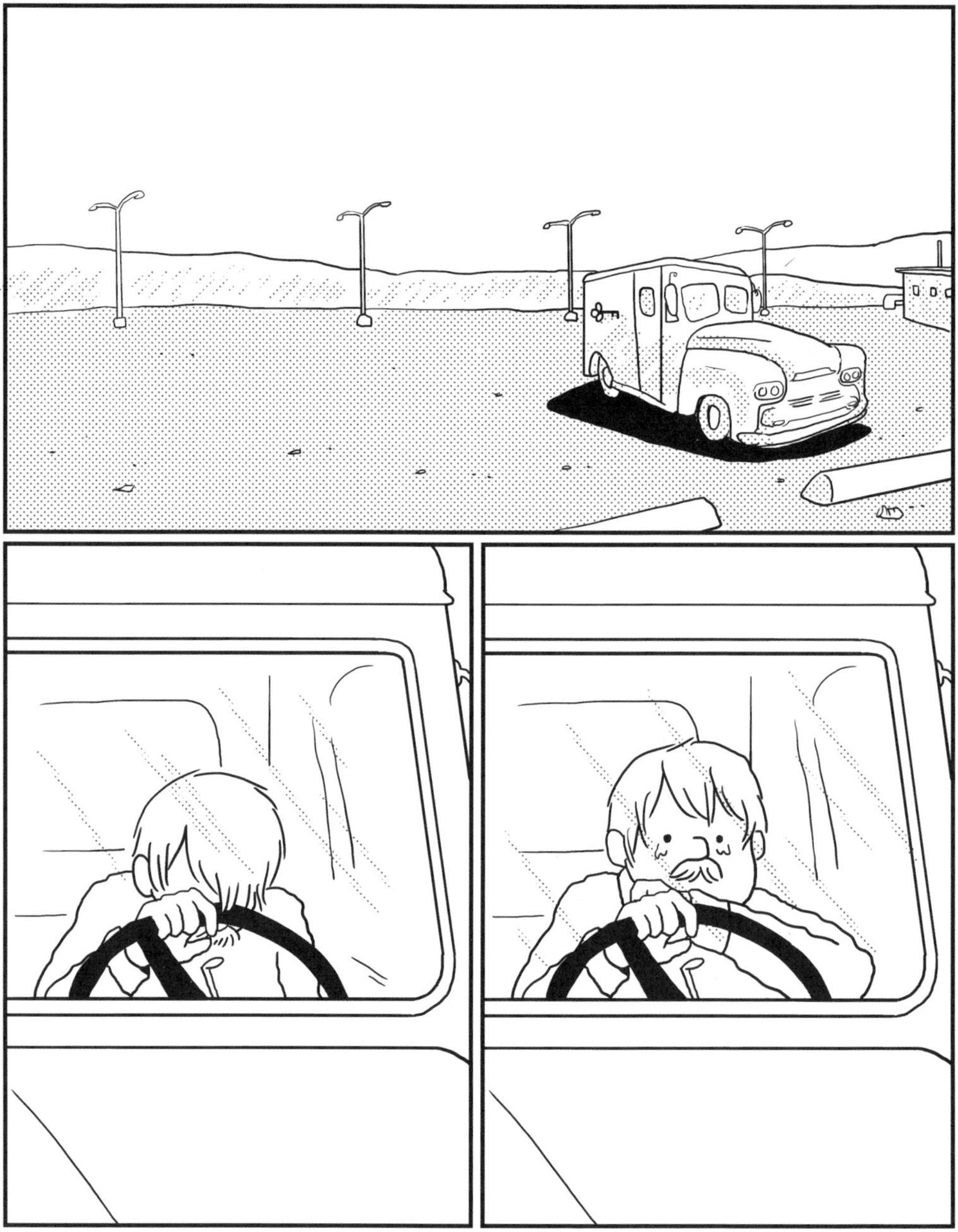

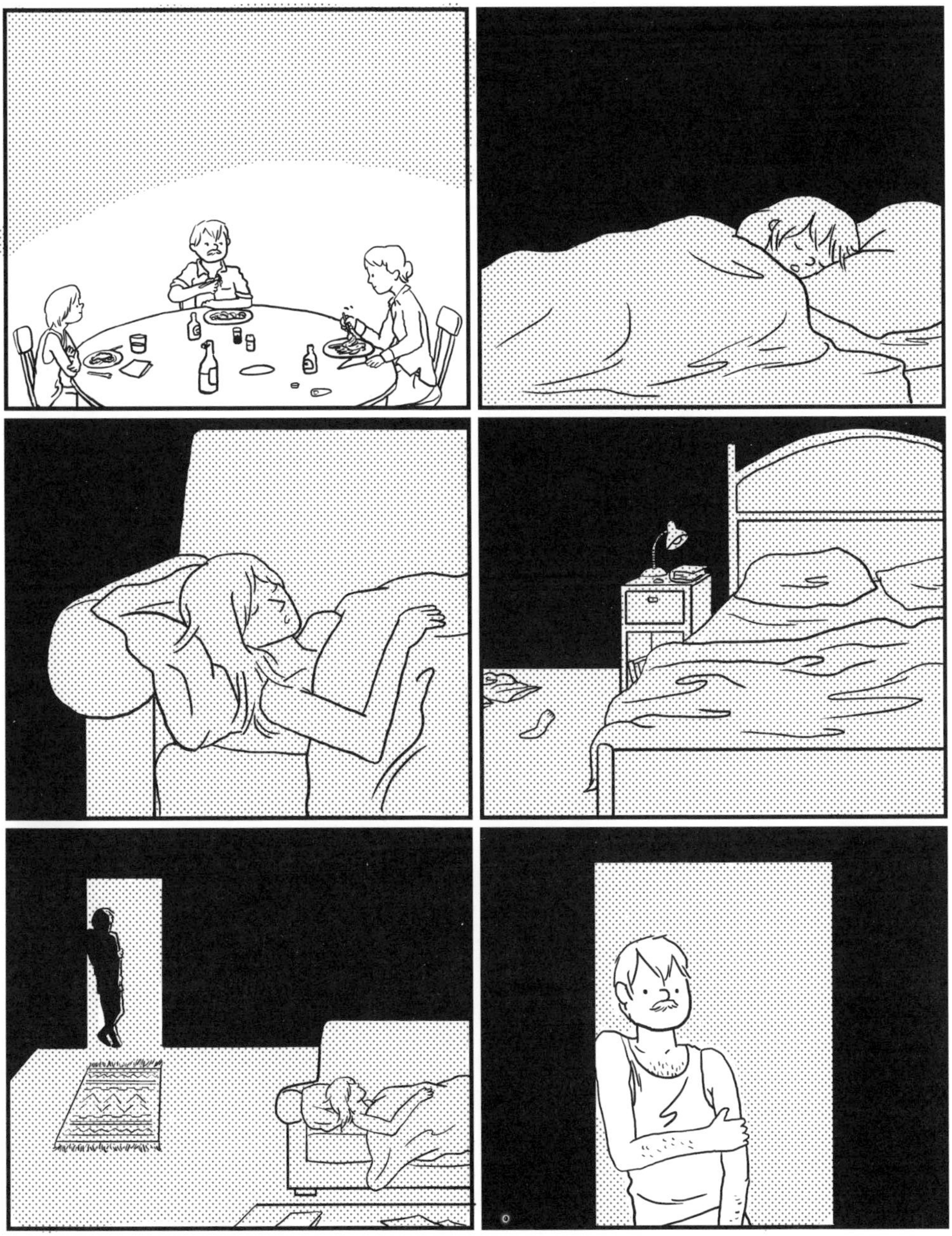

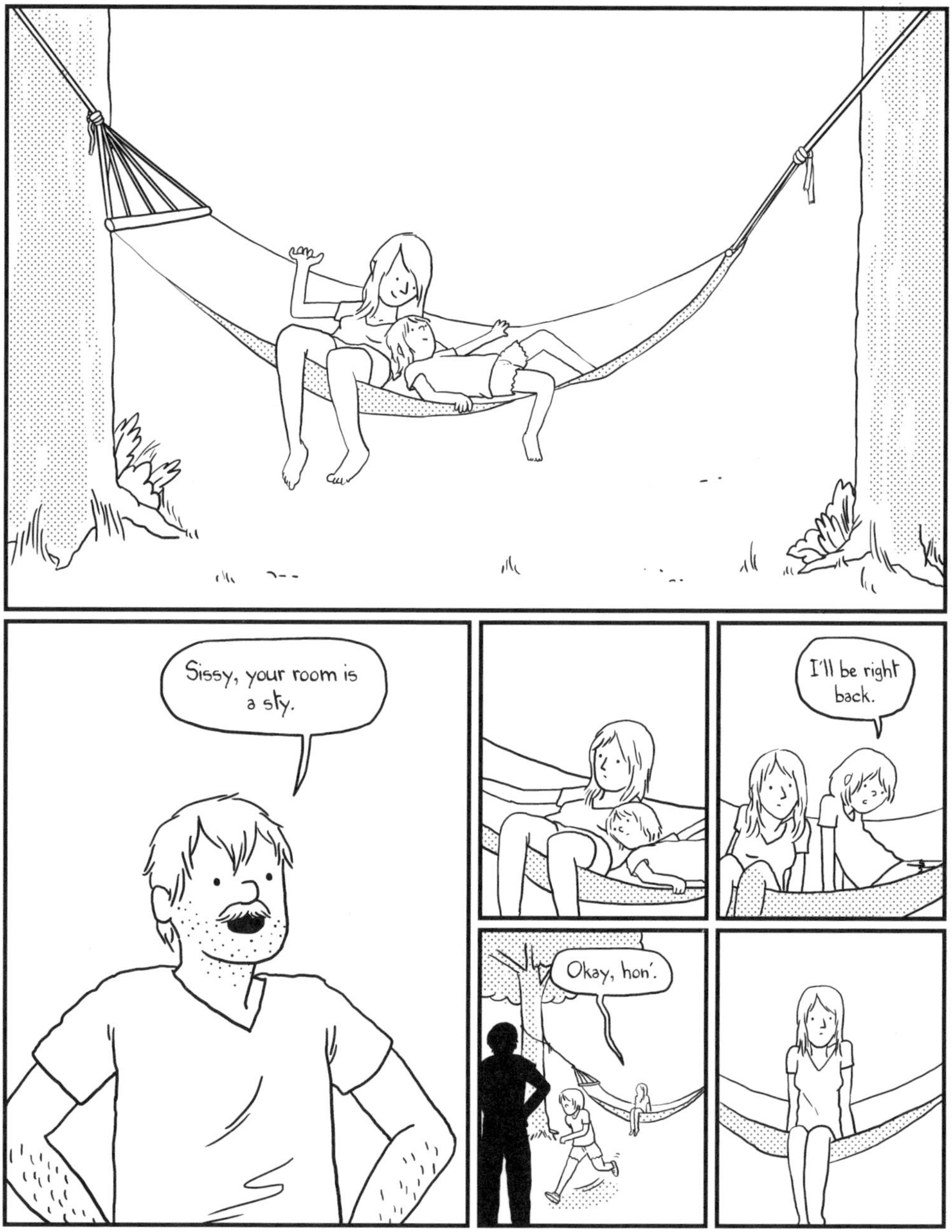
Sissy, your room is a sty.
I'll be right back.
Okay, hon'.

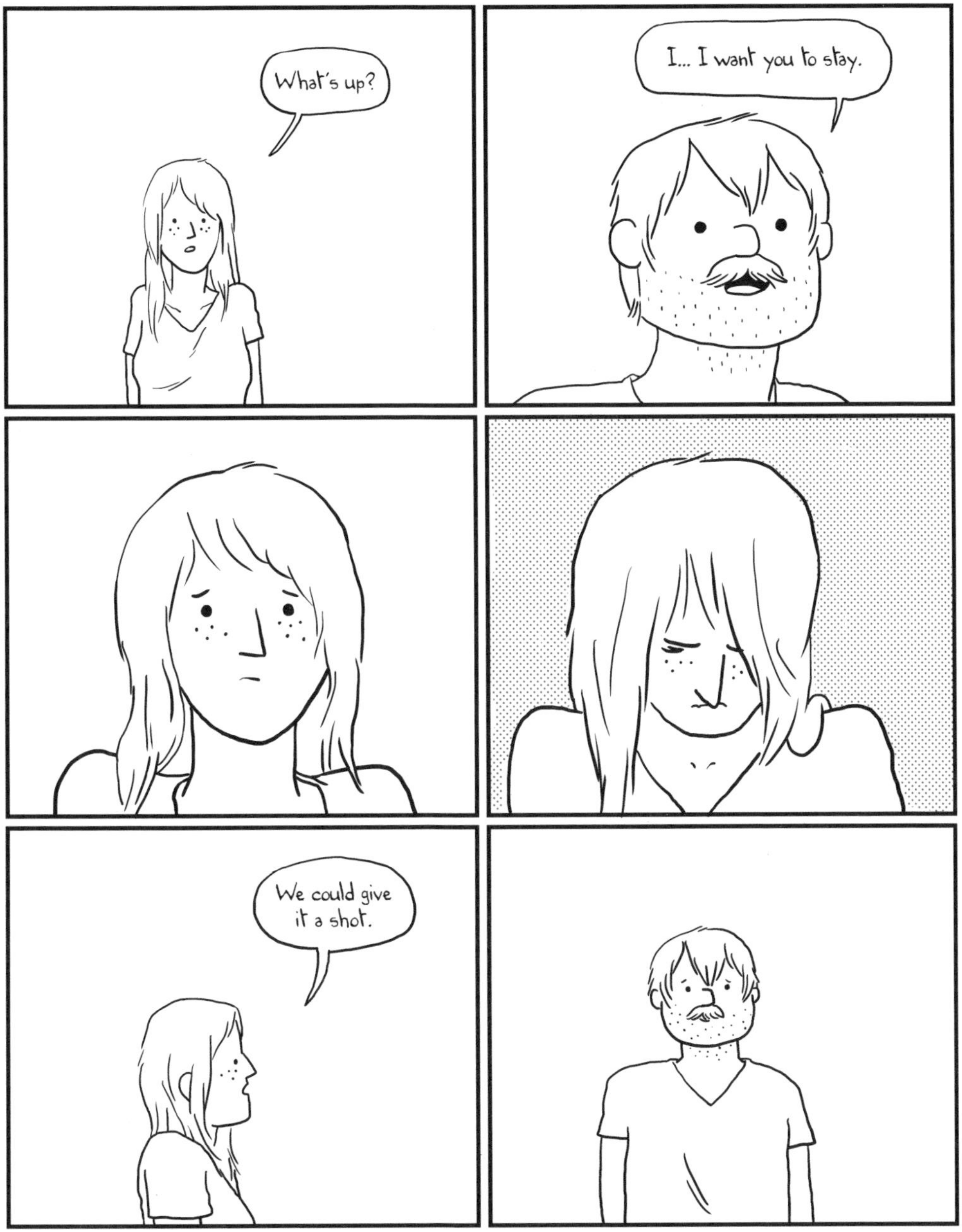
What's up?
I... I want you to stay.
We could give it a shot.

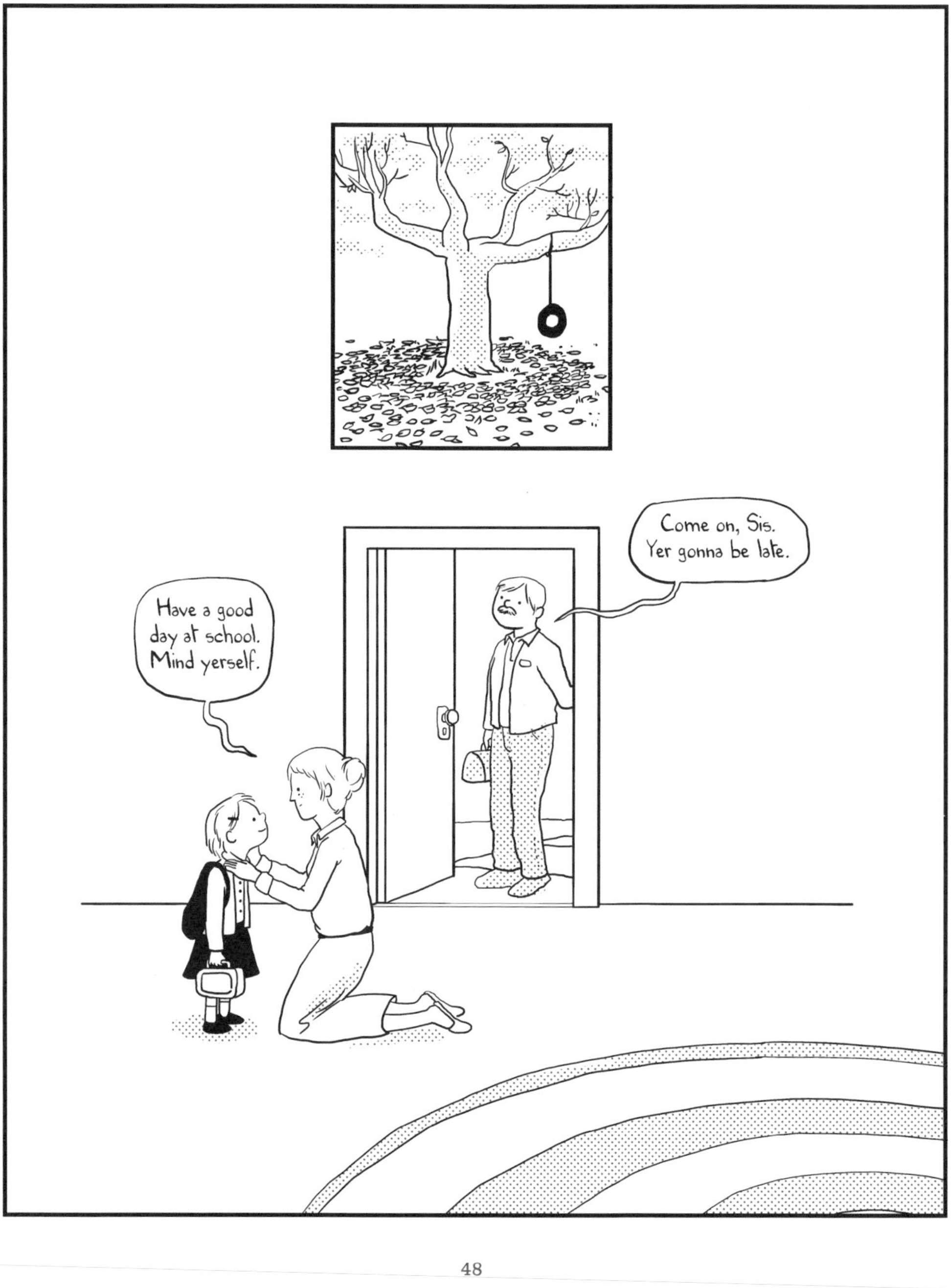
Have a good day at school. Mind yerself.
Come on, Sis. Yer gonna be late.

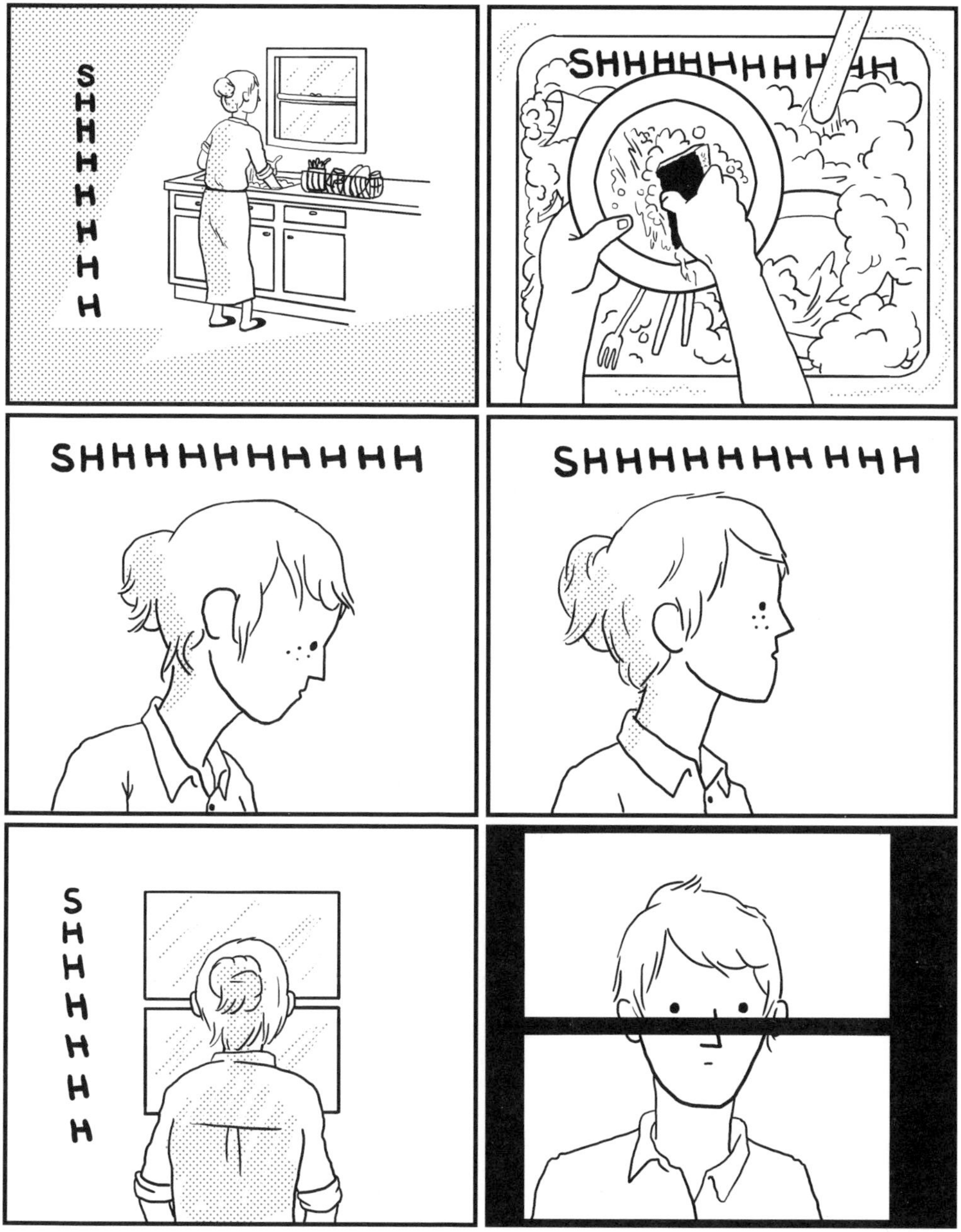
SHHHHHHH
SHHHHHHHHHH
SHHHHHHHHHHH
SHHHHHHHHHHH
SHHHHHHH

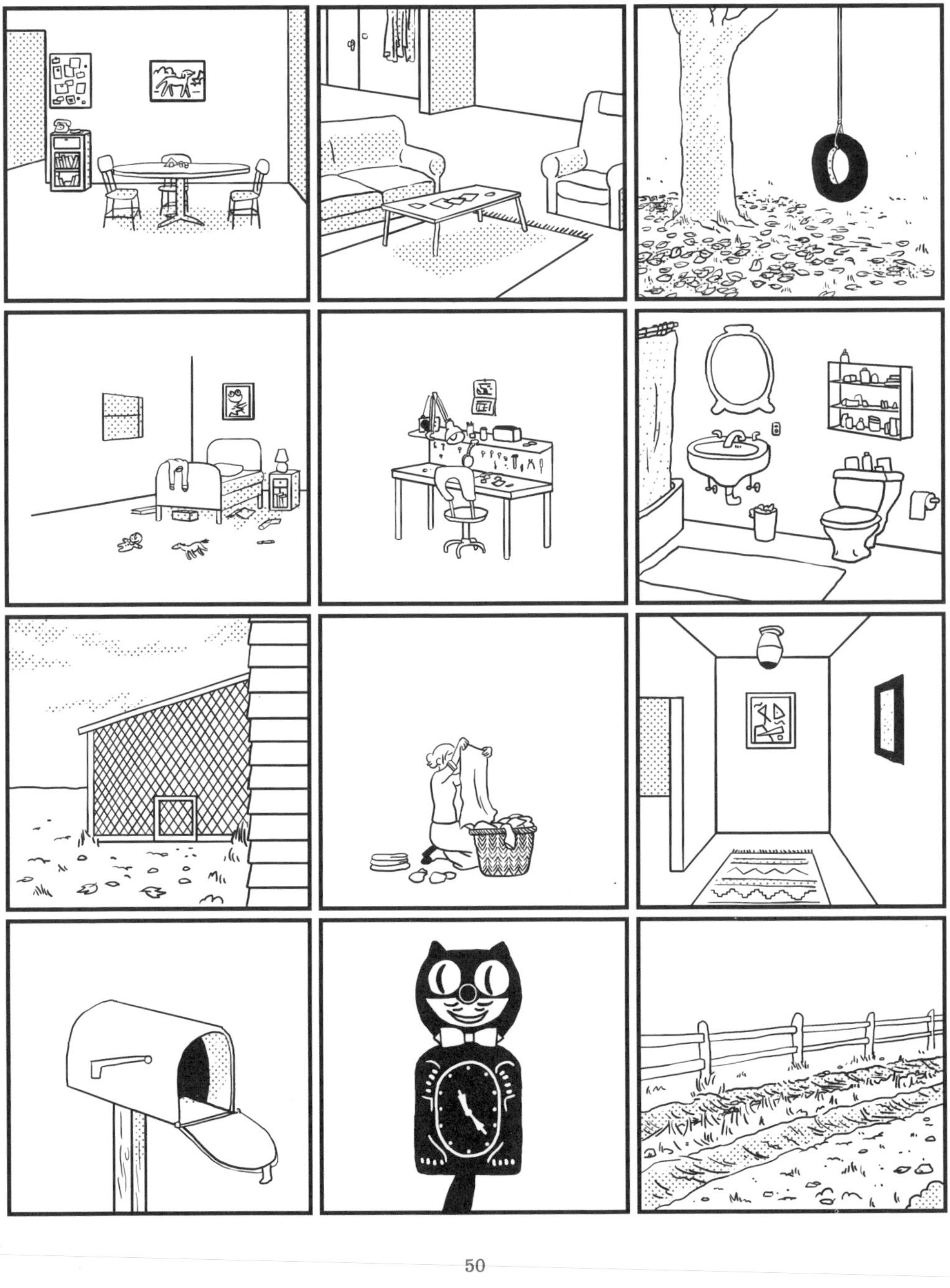

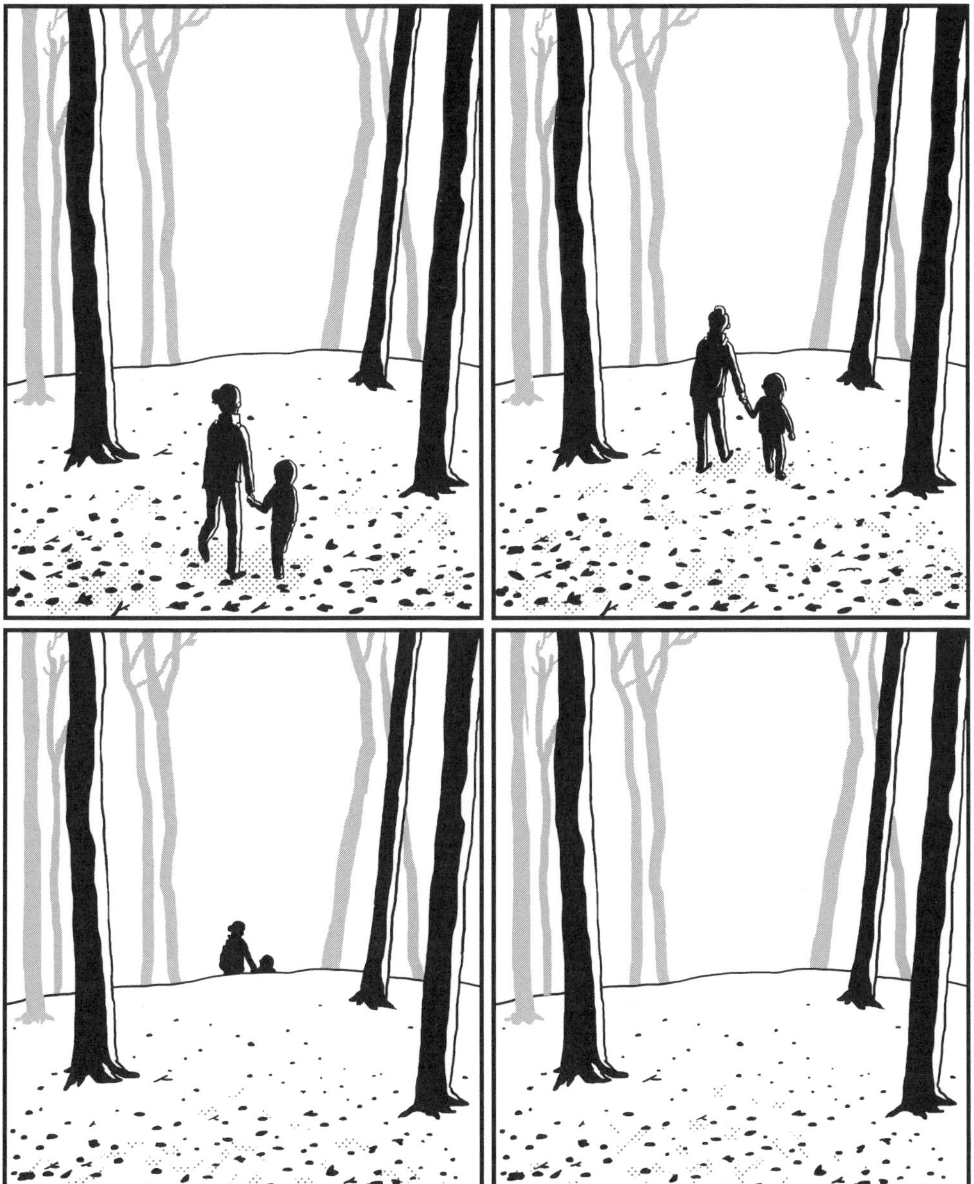

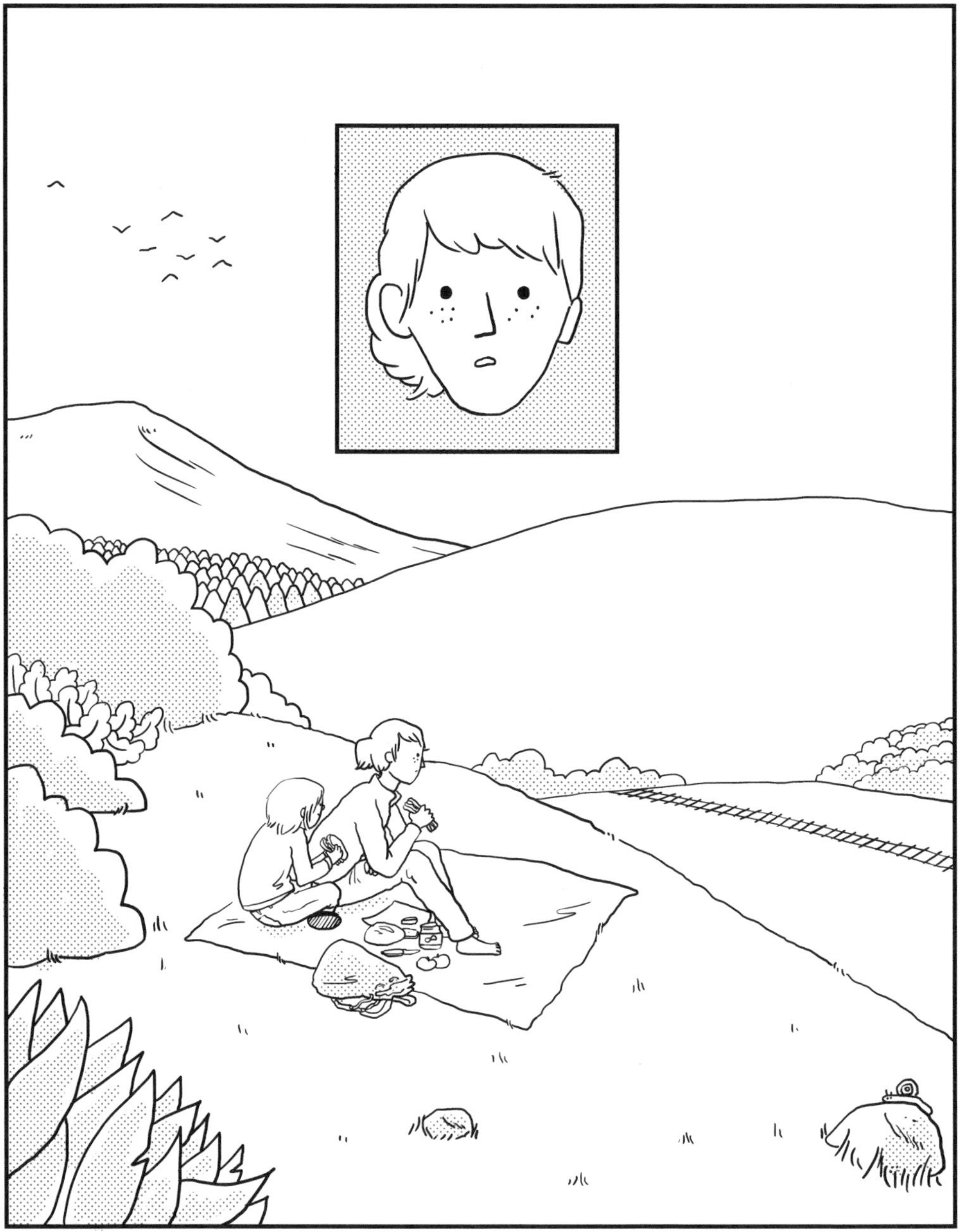

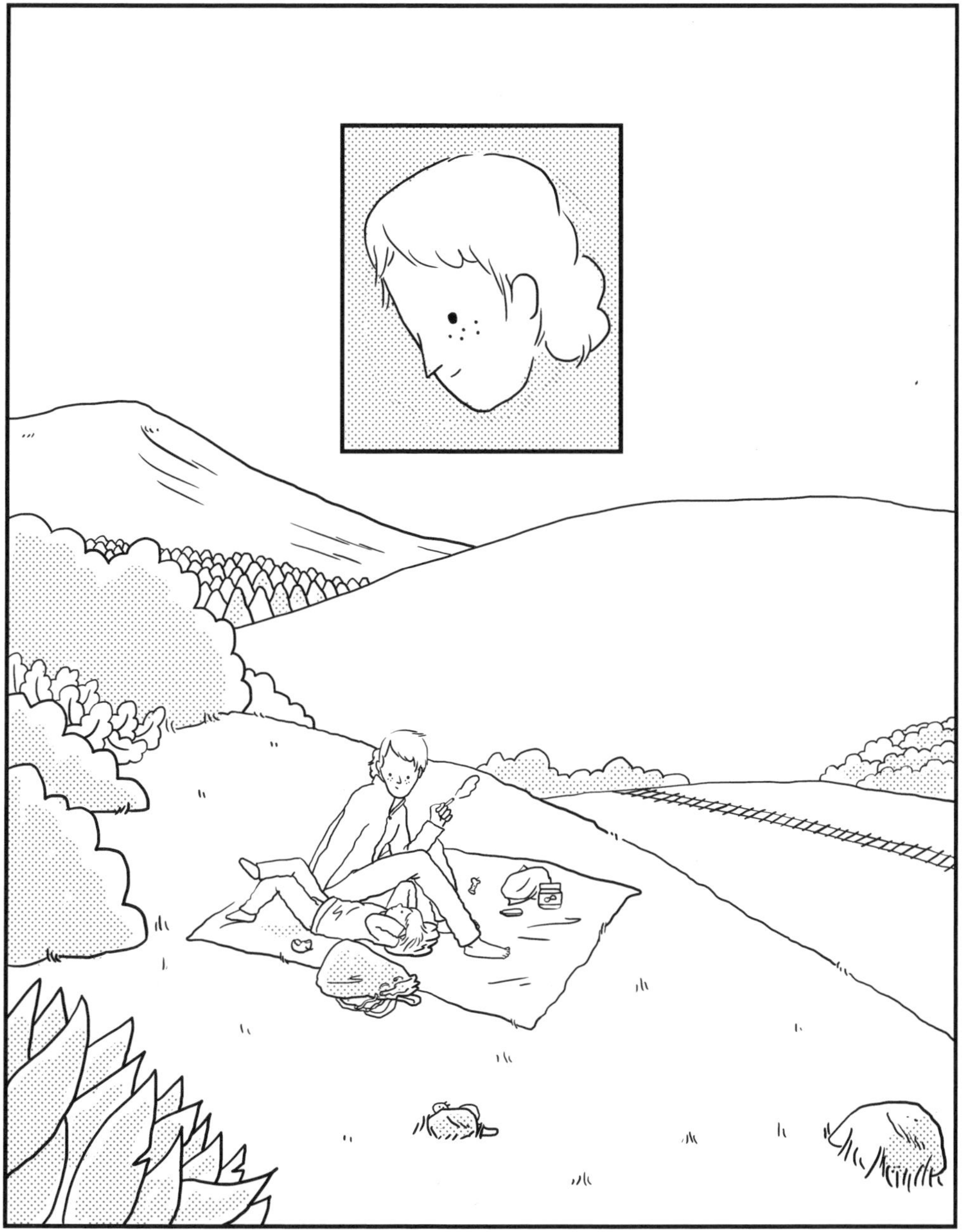

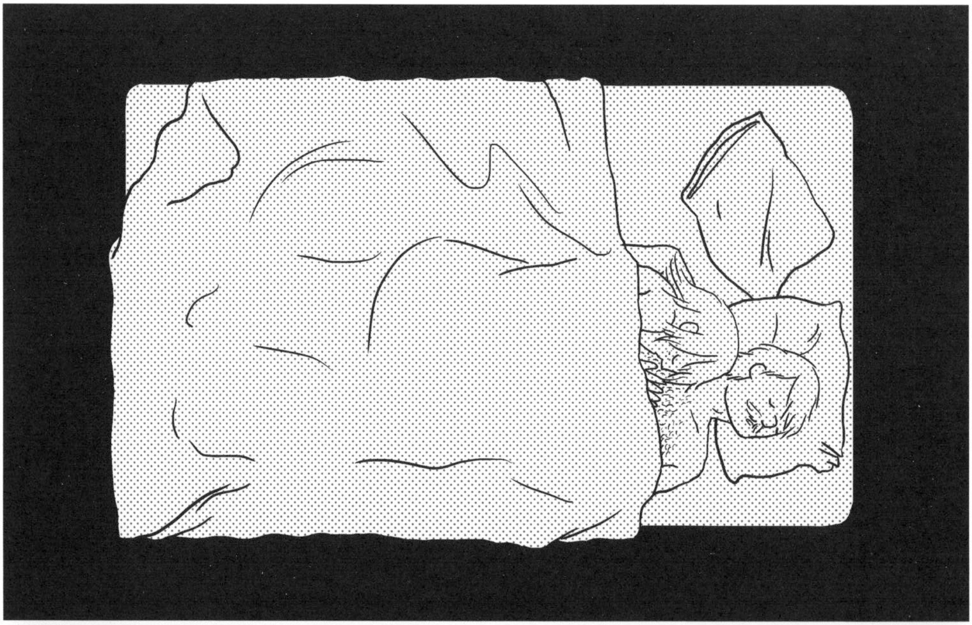

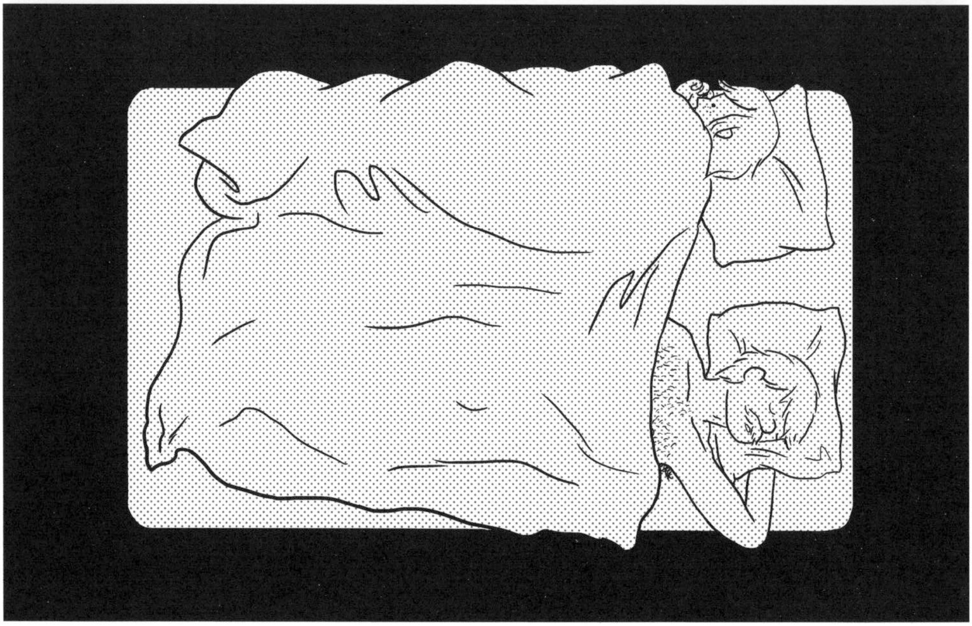

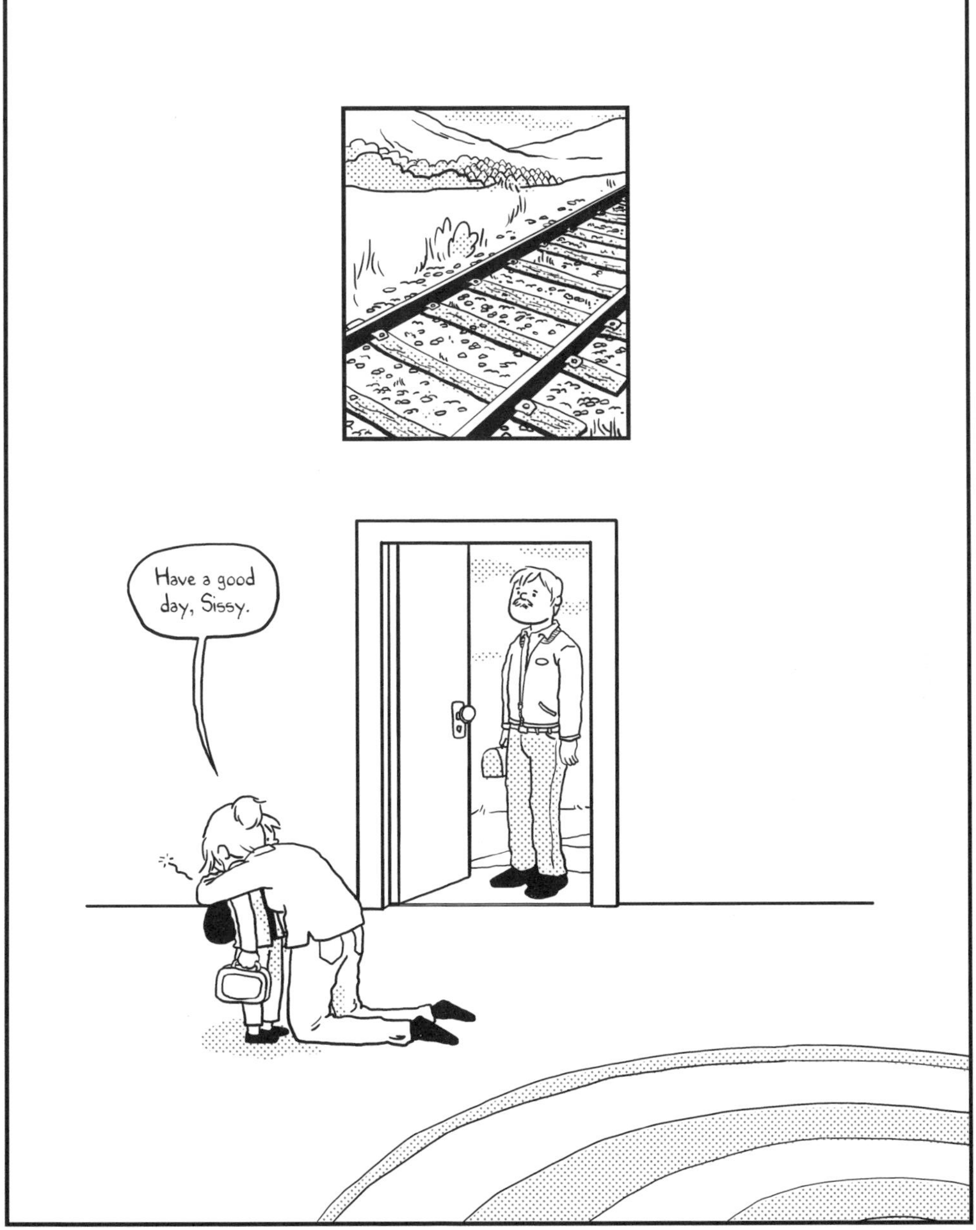
Have a good day, Sissy.

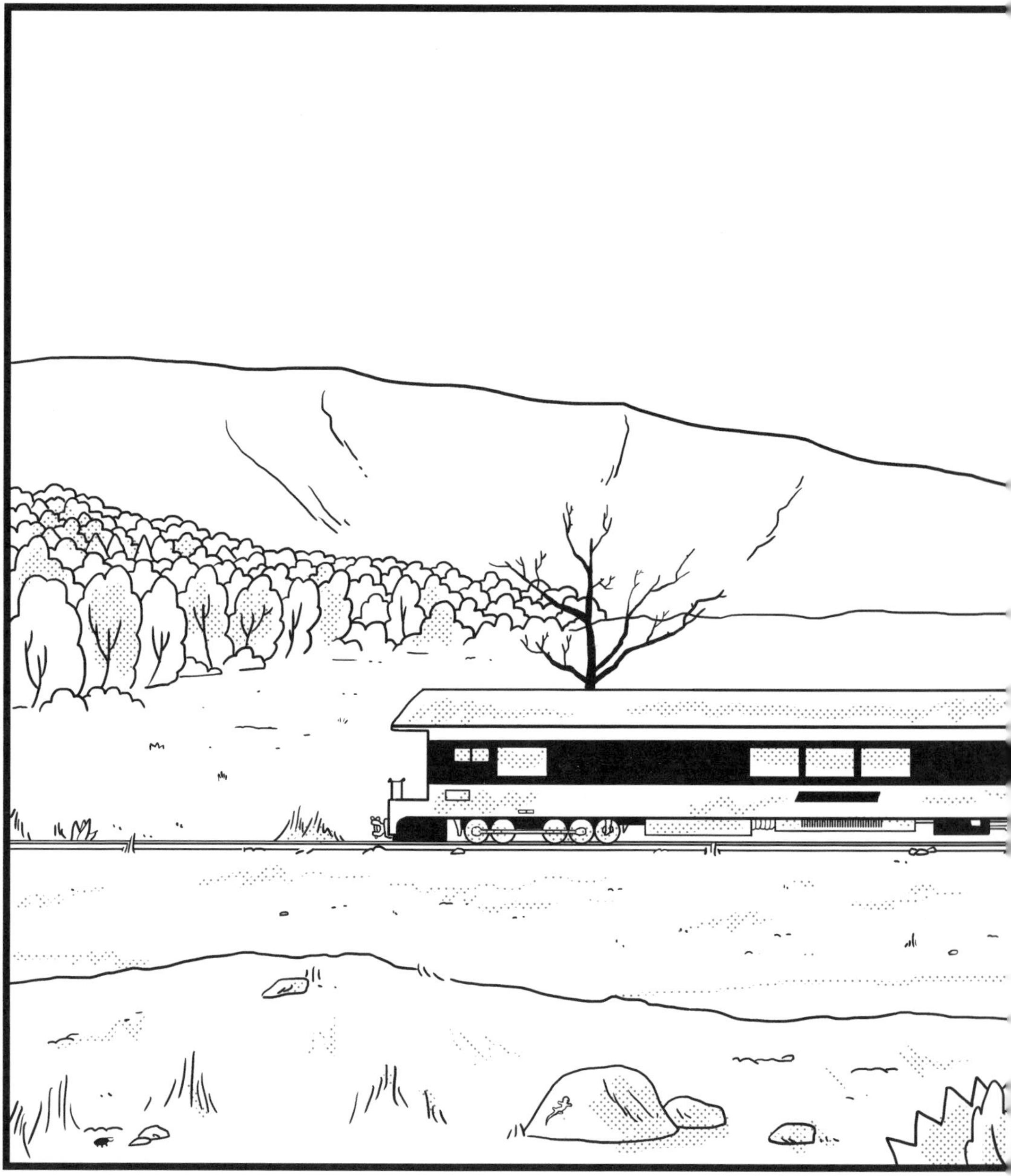

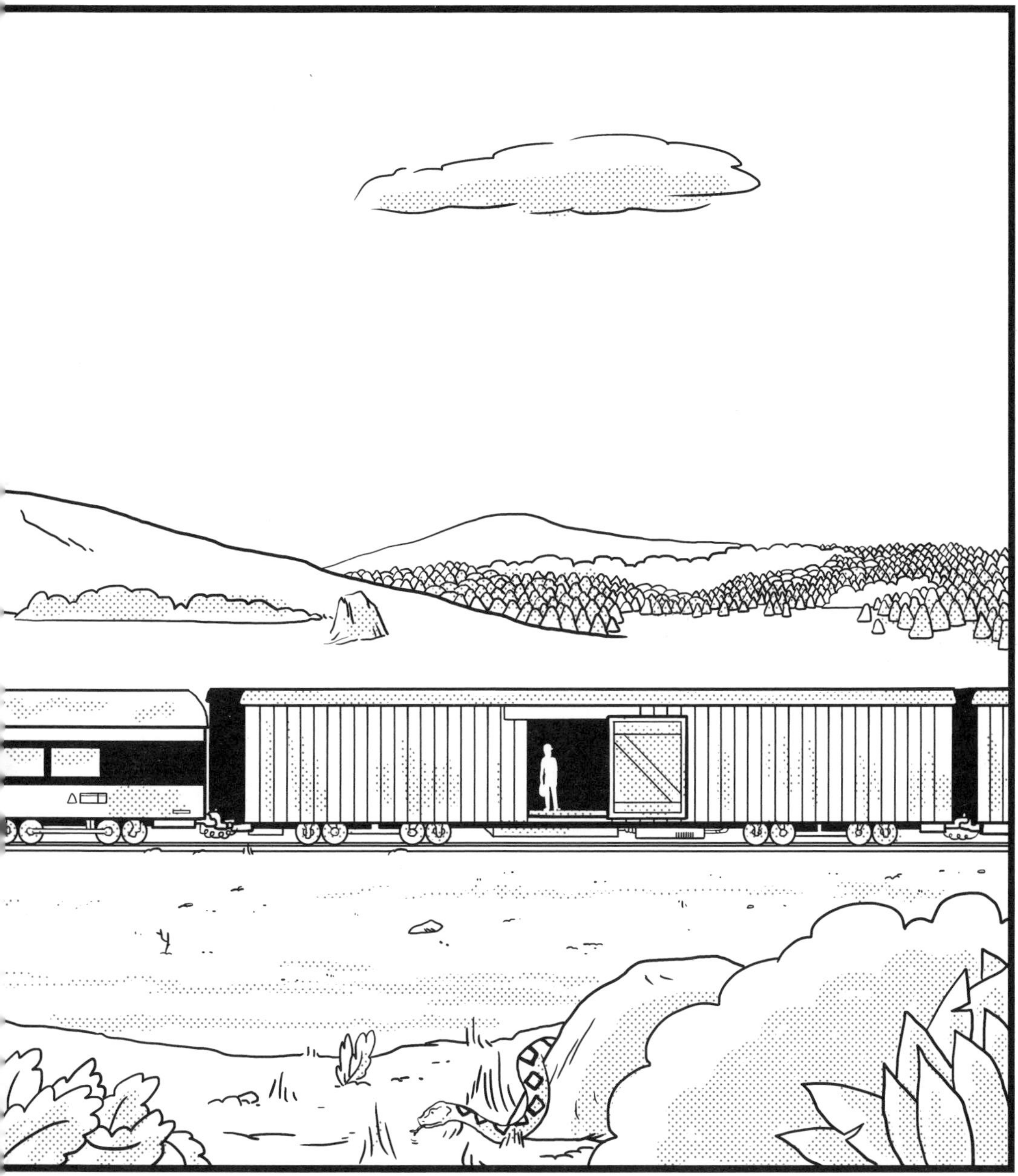

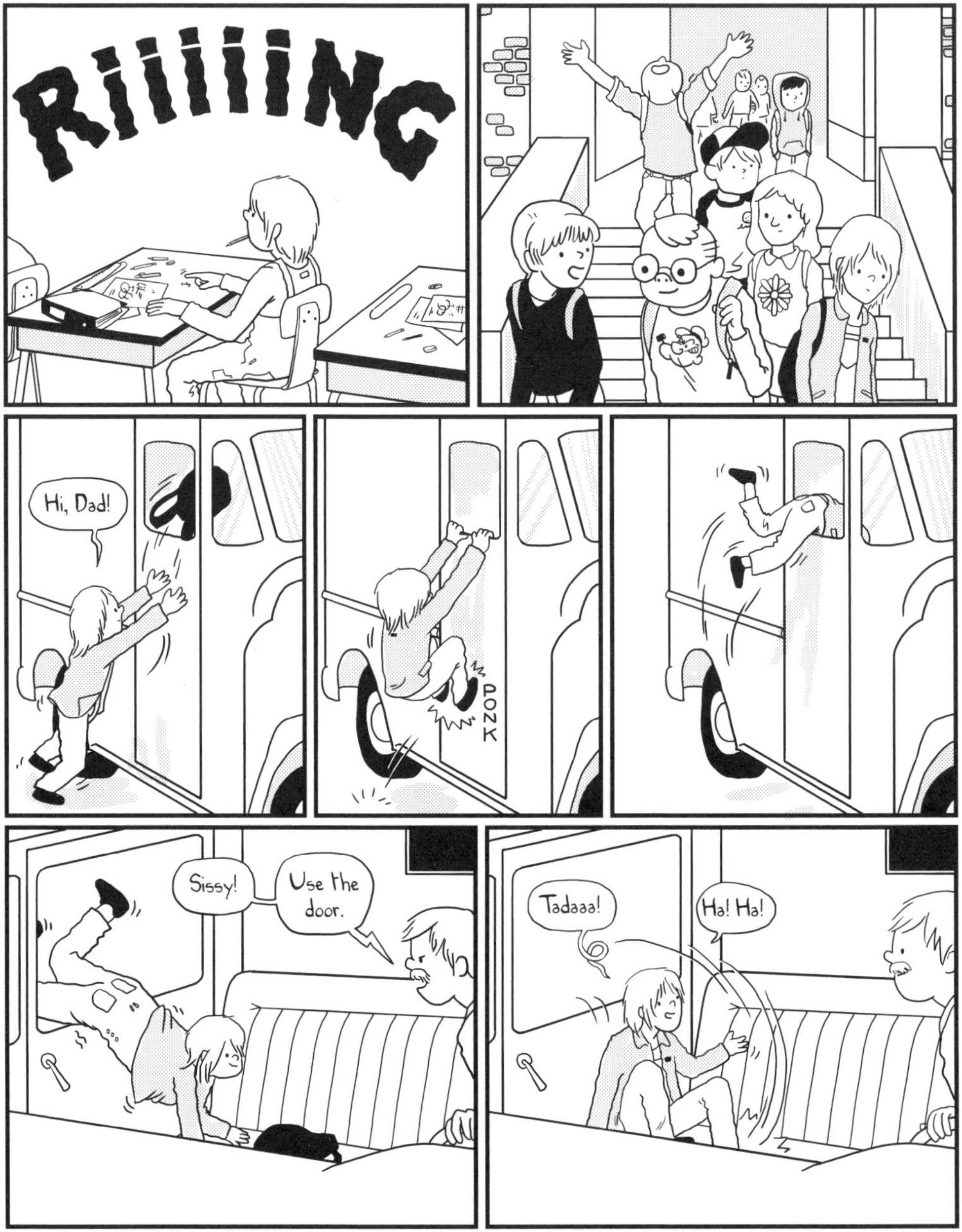

RIIIIING
Hi, Dad!
PONK
Sissy!
Use the door.
Tadaaa!
Ha! Ha!

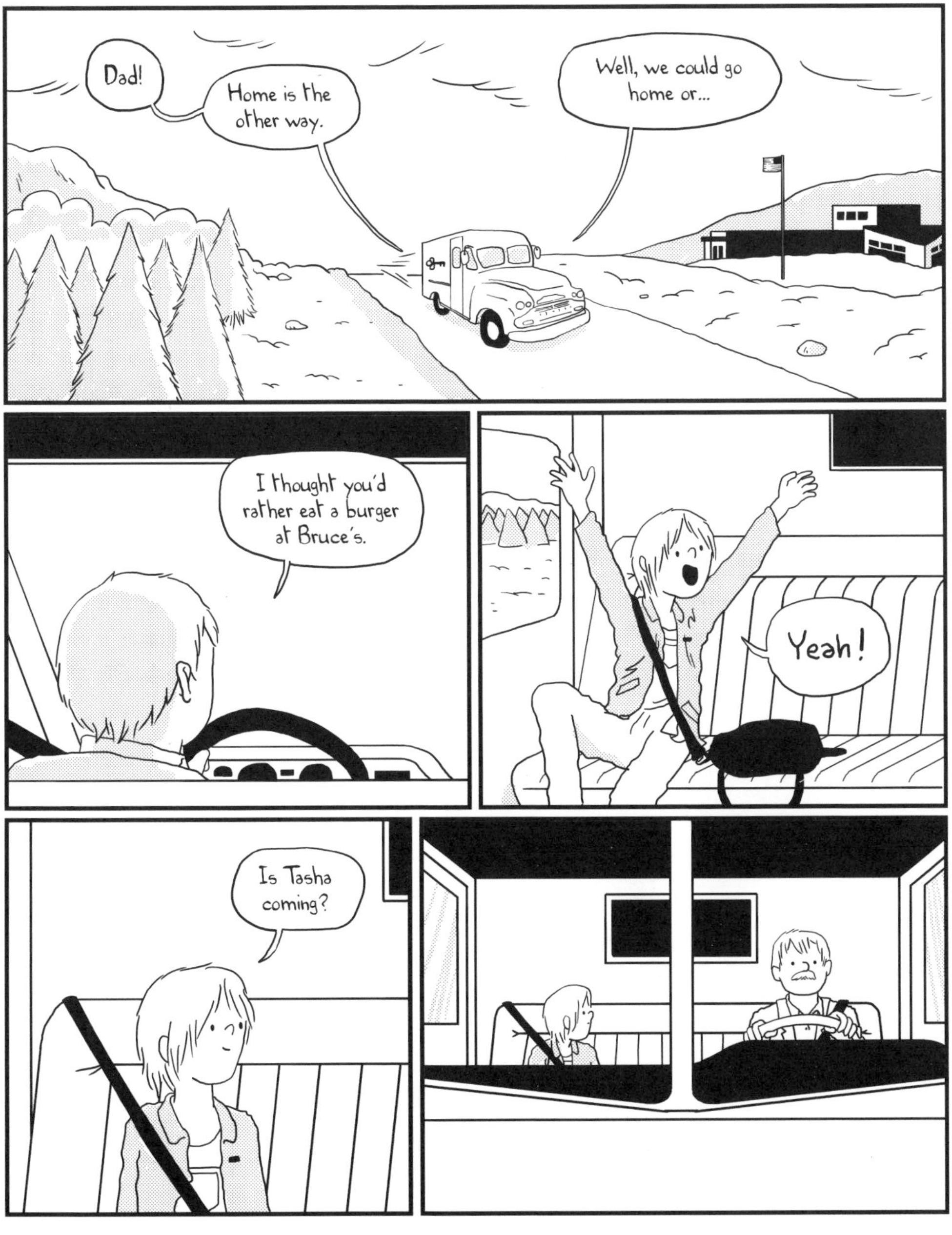
Dad!
Home is the other way.
Well, we could go home or...
I thought you'd rather eat a burger at Bruce's.
Yeah!
Is Tasha coming?

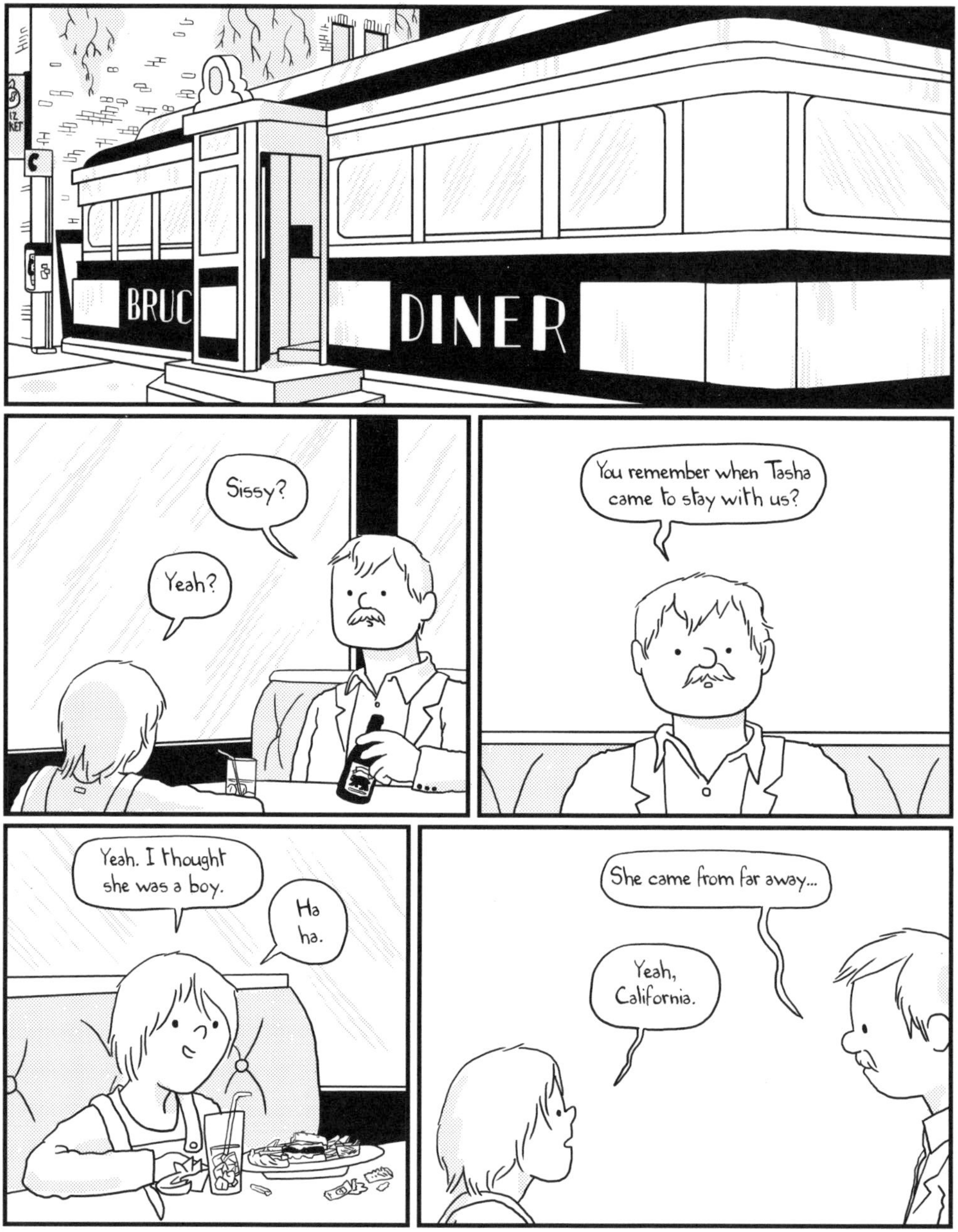
BRUC
DINER
Sissy?
Yeah?
You remember when Tasha came to stay with us?
Yeah. I thought she was a boy.
Ha ha.
She came from far away...
Yeah, California.

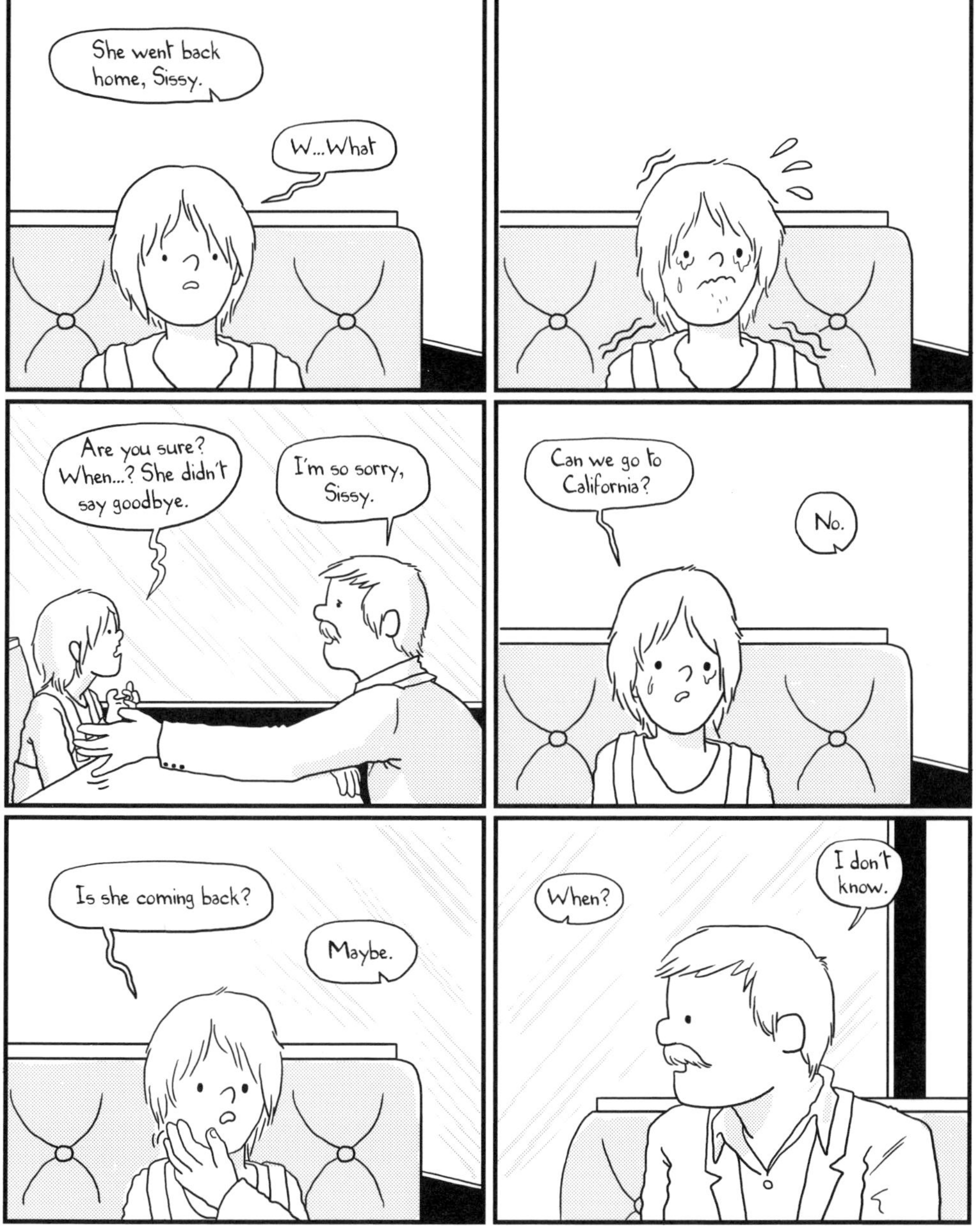
She went back home, Sissy.
W...What
Are you sure? When...? She didn't say goodbye.
I'm so sorry, Sissy.
Can we go to California?
No.
Is she coming back?
Maybe.
When?
I don't know.

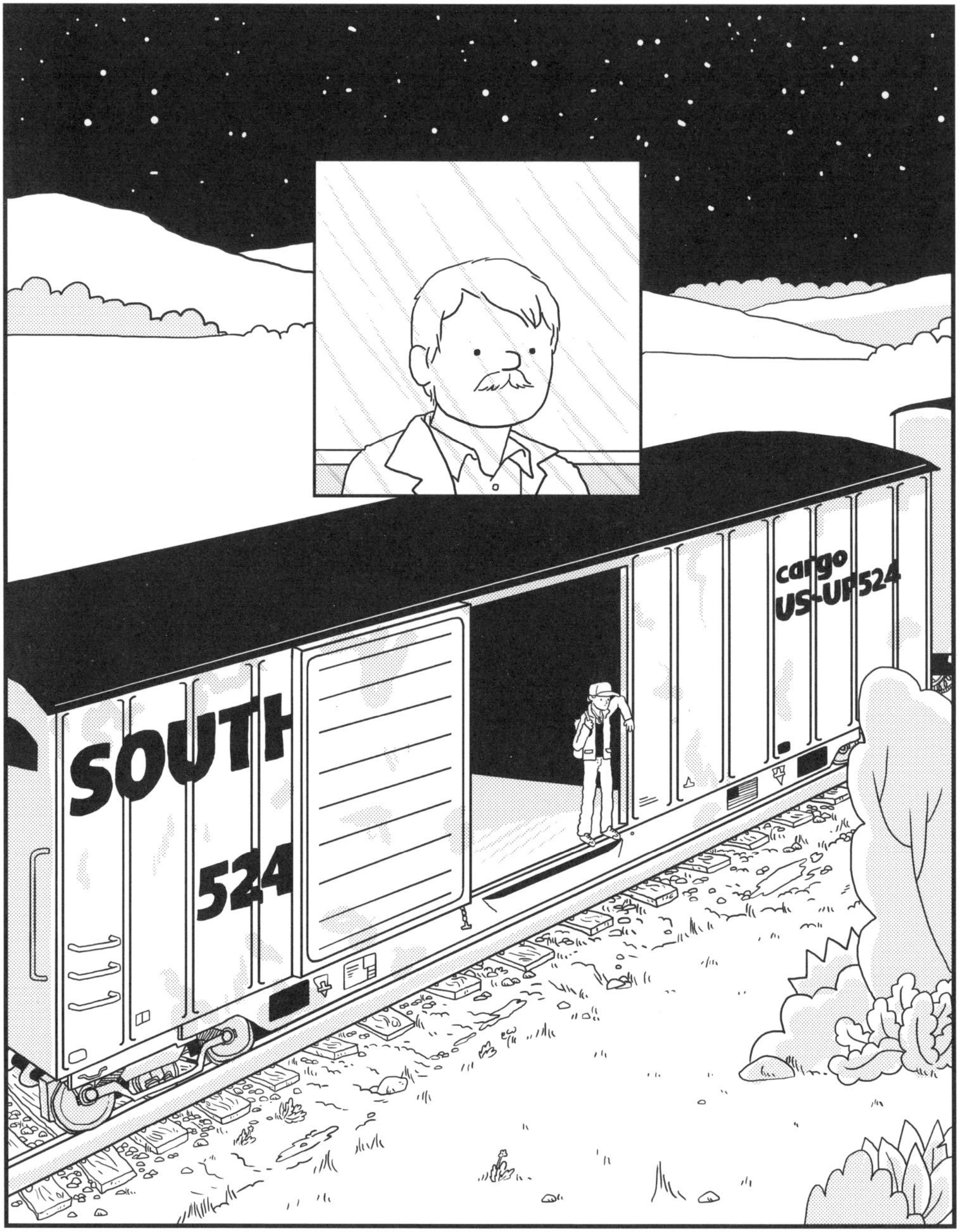
cargo
US-UP524
SOUTH
524

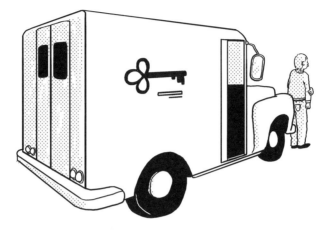

FANTAGRAPHICS BOOKS INC.
7563 Lake City Way NE
Seattle, Washington, 98115

Editor and Associate Publisher: Eric Reynolds
Book Design: Charles Forsman and Max de Radiguès
Cover Design: Charles Forsman, Max de Radiguès, and Justin Allan-Spencer
Production: Paul Baresh
Publisher: Gary Groth

ISBN 978-1-68396-176-5

Library of Congress Control Number: 2018949687
Printed in China

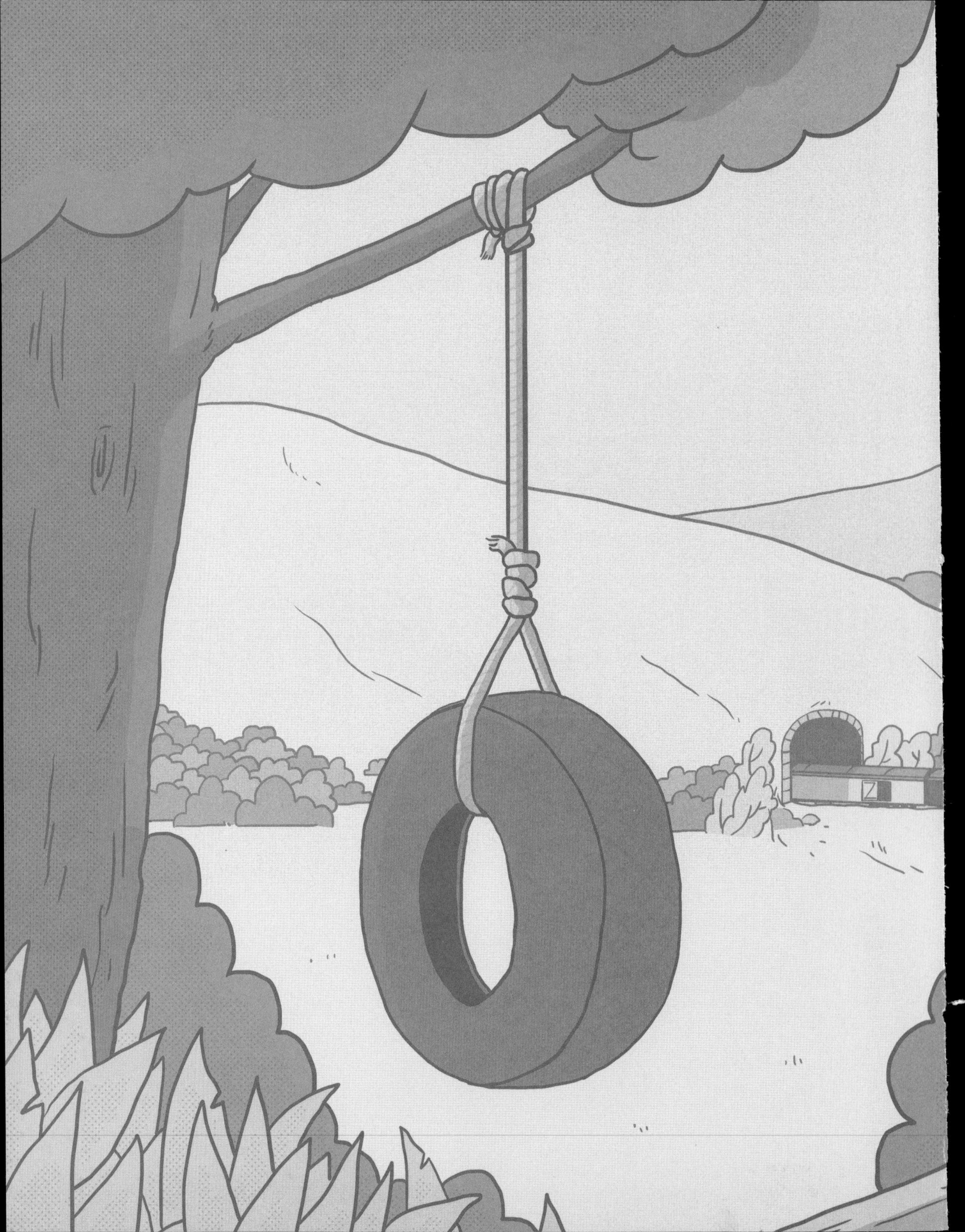
Z